LEADING WITH PASSION AND GRACE

Encouraging and Mentoring Women Leaders in the Body of Christ

Foreword by
Bishop LaDonna C. Osborn, D. Min.

Joyce Strong

Xulon Press
11350 Random Hills Road
Suite 800
Fairfax, VA 22030
(703) 279-6511
XulonPress.com

To order additional copies, call 1-866-909-BOOK (2665).

Table of Contents

SECTION ONE: ANSWERING THE CALL

SECTION TWO: BUILDING A STRONG FOUNDATION

SECTION THREE: ENCOUNTERING CHALLENGES

SECTION FOUR: EMBRACING THE JOURNEY

Foreword

God came to earth in Jesus Christ to redeem humankind from the bondage of sin and to restore women and men to His original plan. The creation account in the book of Genesis reveals that God's human creation—both women and men—were designed to be leaders, to reproduce, to make decisions, to govern, and to administer His program in the earth. Christ accomplished His mission; God's plan can now be fulfilled in and through the life of every person who believes in Him. Leadership is part of the destiny of every Christian.

From the First Century to this Twenty-first Century, redeemed women have been struggling against the effects of sin to reclaim all that Christ has provided for them. They have often been excluded from the positions and functions of leadership. But women of faith have persevered because of their devotion to Christ and His cause. Their journey has not been easy; the challenge continues; progress is evident. Today, Christian women in practically every nation of the world are rising to their full stature in Christ as leaders in the Church and in all areas of Christian ministry.

Joyce Strong is one of those remarkable Christian women who is demonstrating that *with God nothing will be impossible.*Luke 1:37 NKJV She is sharing her experience, her knowledge, and her influence to challenge and equip other women to realize their full potential in their worlds of influence. In her book, *Leading With Passion and Grace,* Reverend Joyce Strong presents a much-needed and valuable resource to teach women (and men) the fundamental skills and the passionate heart of true leadership. The principles that are set forth in this book will empower the Christian leader to survive the discouragements and distractions that often destroy many leaders. Spiritual priorities and practical realities are balanced in this refreshing and systematic approach to leadership.

May Christian leaders—both women and men—strive to fulfill their callings, motivated by Christ's *passion* and governed by God's *grace*.

– Bishop LaDonna C. Osborn, D.Min.

Preface

As we begin this new millennium, women leaders in the Body of Christ are calling for more intentional ministry mentoring. In response to this need, *Leading with Passion and Grace* has been written to encourage and train those who lead in ministry—whether as volunteers or salaried employees—to do so more effectively and wisely.

We all have much to learn in order to employ with excellence the unique qualities and giftings that we bring to the leadership scene. In a culture that is crying *for connectedness, vulnerability and authenticity,* we come particularly qualified, *if* we have become whole in the arms of God and heed the lessons of those who have gone before us.

It is my prayer that present and future female leaders around the world will welcome this book and not only let it speak to us individually, but will also dialog with one another in small groups and seminars so that we can learn from each other's journey.

May we gain strength and wisdom as we yield to the refining of God that always precedes ministry that endures. In the exciting and momentous days ahead, may we lead with passion and grace, bringing glory to the King of Kings.

Introduction

Godly leaders are neither born nor made, but rise from the steady flame of reflection, a longing for meaningful change, great courage and a history of shouldering responsibility and honoring others. Forever fueling the flame is a passionate love for God and a gracious sensitivity to His people.

As that flame leaps higher, we dream unforgettable dreams of a better world and a more effective church. However, as we sense the heat and intensity of the fire within the dream, we realize that we must dream with our eyes wide open, seeing realistically the challenges and dangers and knowing that it will be no easy road.

Between dreams, while we watch the drama of others' lives as well as our own—in the church and on the street—we try to sort out what works and what doesn't, what harms and what heals in the fire of the ways in which men and women lead. As we seek God, our passion burns deep—yielding a gritty determination to do it well, for the gospel's sake and our love for God.

In the waiting for opportunity, we may press ahead prematurely, thinking we know the disciplined flame of leadership better than anyone, only to find that our greatest lessons are to be learned through failure. At such times, we think all is lost and the passion threatens to abandon us. But, amazingly, after we have been consumed by the Refiner's fire, our dreams lying in ashes, *God* opens the doors to serious leadership and even places young dreamers under our care! At first we doubt our ability to lead or equip *anyone*—remembering our weaknesses and our own stumbling in the past—but then the Spirit stirs the fires of passion for His work once again. And, like Moses hearing God's call in the wilderness, we cry out, "Yes, Lord, but I will not go unless You go with me!" When this happens, our passion is at last tempered by grace...and we are ready to move in *His* power and humility.

Section One:

ANSWERING THE CALL

Chapter One

THE ROOT OF OUR PASSION

For Christ's love compels us...
2 Cor. 5:14

God authors dreams of what is not yet, but should be. He awakens us with visions of ministry that will radically change lives and build an eternal Kingdom, while whispering into our spirits the call to make a specific difference in the world.

As these visions come into focus and the call rings true, passion to bring them into reality grabs hold of our hearts. This passion then becomes the fuel that propels us forward, filling us with an amazing energy. Passion will cause the visions to burn in our bones, bringing us ownership and making us care to the point of tears and great sacrifice. If we lack deep and driving conviction for the cause, our strength will give out under pressure, and all those we have influenced will falter. Passion is essential.

THE POWER OF PASSION

. I love being around passionate leaders. They can inspire me to catch the vision they so fervently espouse and make me want to stretch to do something about it. They are able to paint a vivid picture of a better world and challenge me to rally my giftings, asking God to use me in every way possible. And at those times when my own spiritual dreams have seemingly died, merely being in the presence of a deeply passionate person who has faith to move mountains can cause those dreams to spring once more to life. Hope and purpose are rekindled. What power there is in passion!

However, I've learned to be wary of such people as well. Passionate leaders can seduce followers to commit insane acts—even in the name of God—as witnessed by Rev. Jim Jones' power over his congregation that led them to commit mass suicide in the jungles of Guyana several years ago. Passionate leaders can also infuse us with ulterior motives and cause us to violate principle after principle in the name of a just cause. Passion can be devilishly convincing and intoxicating. Therefore, passion alone is not a safe indicator of the fire of God in the heart of a leader.

Passion must be tested. Not all passion takes us to higher ground.

SELF-SERVING PASSION

When I began teaching many years ago at Teen Challenge Training Center, a male, residential discipleship program for ex-drug addicts and alcoholics, I too was surely passionate. I thought at the time that my boundless energy was solely for the salvation and growth of my students, and I gratefully embraced their appreciative and affirming responses to my teaching and leadership style. But in time, I discovered that my passion for their spiritual success was laced with my own hunger for approval.

Passion rooted in human need or desire will never yield authentic spiritual leadership.

A REVELATION

So what *should be* the source of our passion in ministry? In our best moments, what should be the force that drives us to press on in spite of every conceivable difficulty? Will a worthy cause provide us with enough energy to stay the course with integrity?

While watching the delightful movie, ***The Princess Bride***—a tale set in some obscure European country in medieval times—I was amazed to hear the answer to these questions in just two words. For you who have not yet seen the movie, the moment of revelation came when the fallen hero, Wesley, was taken by his two friends to Miracle Max for a cure that would restore his life.

Miracle Max put a bellows into Wesley's mouth and began pumping air into the mostly-dead man's lungs. After three powerful pumps, Miracle Max leaned over him and yelled, "Hey, down there. What'cha got that's worth living for?" as his hands pushed forcefully down on Wesley's chest.

As Max bent down to catch Wesley's answer—and all others in the cottage held their breath—these words came weakly from the young man's mouth: "True love!"[1]

At that, I jumped up from the couch in my living room where I had been watching the movie and shouted, "That's it! *True love*." Of course, I didn't mean the true love of a man for a woman, but rather the *true love of God for mankind!* That alone should be the fire in our bones and our reason for responding to His call to lead. That alone will give us courage to face the devils in the fire swamps of the human heart and keep us true to our convictions.

WHERE IT ALL BEGAN

How well we remember the day that God first touched our hearts with His *true love*—forgiving and cleansing us! We have never been the same since! It's because He first *loved* us that we burn with passion for Him and long to take His message to the world, following the dreams He has planted in our hearts. *True love*–that which will pay any price for another's redemption–came to us by the gift of Jesus' life, and now that very life within us reaches out to love others.

It's a miracle! We love because He first loved us...and *that* love inspires us, challenges us, graces and comforts us as we follow in His footsteps into the uncharted jungle of ministry leadership.

Our need for His *true love* will never end. We would lose all sense of direction without it! Fresh encounters with Him—in which we are purified and set right again, our motive for Christian service and leadership refined—will be our mainstay on the battlefield, keeping us from disgrace. Without poignant visitations of *true love* in His presence, we will very quickly revert to serving out of what Henri Nouwen, in his book, *In the Name of Jesus*, calls "Second Love." By that he means the love of ourselves...to bring ourselves praise; to be heroes; to garner power and prestige; or even to cause others to be dependent upon us. Such love is far from *true*.

THE BURNING QUESTION

The Apostle Peter's encounter with Jesus after His resurrection was amazing in its challenge. Remember the question Jesus posed? He asked Peter three times, "Do you love me?" adding the third time, "...more than these?" I believe Jesus was after something profoundly necessary before He could commission Peter to "Feed my sheep."

Peter was *already* painfully–and gratefully–aware of *Jesus' love for him* after being forgiven for betraying his Lord, but Jesus knew that it was one thing to *receive* the selfless love of God, but quite another to return it. This was the final test: How much did Peter love Jesus in return? Did there remain any danger that Peter would place ahead of his service to Jesus his love for someone or something else? Was it still possible that the passionate fisherman turned preacher could be deterred from the mission if he were offended or if times got tough?

Becoming a spokesman for a cause that would strike at the very gates of hell would require Peter to lay aside self-protection, release control of his own life and plunge headlong into a life of moment-by-moment trust in the One Who had given His life for him. Only if Peter entered into a love affair with his Lord—loving Him above all else—would he be an effective leader in the critical days ahead. If

Peter's love were tentative or self centered, Jesus knew that he would not possess the inner confidence to take correction, be held accountable, or be brave when bound by enemies and taken through painful experiences where he would rather not go. (John 21:15)

The Peter we see later in the Book of Acts and reflected in his own epistles (I and II Peter) is a man who loves with abandonment and walks in an eternal destiny. Because of living and breathing *true love*, he has become an open and vulnerable leader, never afraid to learn from failure. He knows God intimately and trusts His answers even when he doesn't understand. Only because he is secure in his relationship with God can he dare risk his heart and life to preach uncompromisingly to the men and women who would yet kill him.

The same holds true for us today. Jesus asks us the same question: "Do you *love Me*?" Only when we love and trust Him with abandonment and certainty–and more than all else–will we be able to influence others to also love and trust Him with all their hearts. Only then will we lead by *true love*, without hungering for personal power. And only then will we be able to follow Christ through the valleys of disappointment and testing—even deprivation, persecution and the threat of death—and emerge from our own "fire swamps" of adversity still victorious and passionate for the Call.

SIGNS OF MIXED MOTIVES

How will we know when we have slipped into the mire of serving out of 2nd love, a love that mixes service for God with service for our own interests?

1. A tendency to pacify others in order to obtain their approval
2. A need to have our names attached to every victory
3. Fear of vulnerability
4. Competition or jealousy in our hearts regarding others' gifts
5. Possessiveness of the ministry
6. Difficulty in delegating even when we understand the need to do so
7. Fear of losing our position
8. Defensiveness when questioned about an issue or problem

WE NEED HELP

Right from the start, before we influence another soul, we must ask God to direct us each to a mature, spiritually discerning believer whom we can trust and to whom we can tell our life's story. *Who we have come to be, through the experiences in our lives, can play a dramatic role in the way we ultimately lead.*

We must tell this person the truth about ourselves. As we look back over our lives we will see where we have been hurt or belittled, and we can ask him or her to return there with us in prayer to help us forgive the offenders and release them from the judgments we have formed against them. As we forgive, we will be forgiven by the Father and pronounced whole again. Throughout the process, we will see at last that He was carrying us in the arms of love during those dreadful days. We would not have made it to *this* day if He hadn't. (See *Steps to Freedom* in Appendix)

Our own secret sins as well need to be addressed. Behavior for which we have never repented will keep us bound to our guilt— hobbling us like a horse with his front legs tied together—when asked to lead a charge against unrighteousness. When we confess our sins to another, exposure to the light of day destroys their secret control over us. Repentance allows the blood of Jesus to cleanse us and wash those sins away. Hearing another voice echo Jesus' forgiveness settles the issue at long last... and we are free!

When the guilt is gone, we need never again hide for fear of exposure. In the wonderful experience of being forgiven by Him in the presence of one who has heard our confession and pronounced forgiveness, the sin's power over us is broken and shame's shadows are dispelled. No longer must we avoid subjects or ministry that might ferret out our sin and humiliate us. As we acknowledge our sinful past and walk the humbling road of repentance and receive His forgiveness, we will find ourselves free to embrace and help others, who have sinned in the same way, come clean as well.

OUR RELATIONSHIP TO HIM

Only if we continually abide in His life-changing love for us will we be fearlessly obedient in our leadership—even to the death if necessary—in the years to come. Out of our personal, passionate love for God and our gratitude to Him, as well as a keen understanding of our freedom and destiny, we will fashion each mission to introduce the world to *true love* in the person of the life-changing Savior. We will give authentic ministry leadership because it comes out of an intimate *relationship* with God–not a faith in ourselves, in a philosophy or in our abilities.

Because of His sacrifice and His constancy in our lives, we will grow in our knowledge that we are of great value to Him. By His grace—and because we remember His sacrifice for us—we will not seek our identities in what we might *do* for Him or the applause of others, but rather define ourselves by our *relationship* with Him.

If we are not in constant love with God, we will sadly attract the needy only to *us*…and we can save no one. This we must remember all the days of our lives.

We will be held fast to our *true love* as we daily enter His presence in prayer, meditation and worship. His word–both written and spoken into our hearts–and our *honest* conversations with Him will send a taproot down into the strength and power of God for our lives and ministries, yielding the courage to be obedient. As we ask the Holy Spirit daily to fill us, teach us and reveal to us the Father's heart, we will be shaped into His likeness. No one else's passion can give this to us...or take it from us.

It is this love burning within us that will cause our eyes to turn compassionately outward upon the world. As we feel their pain and learn to weep, a keen sense of destiny will begin to grip us and propel us to action.

And as we act, it must be without expectation of immediate return or reward. True leaders learn that they are the first to suffer and the last to take credit. As God serves *us* daily by His presence, we will simply serve others. Those we lead will learn of God's love by receiving it from us first. This love will be the seed sown for a later, larger harvest.

True love will grow during the time we spend at His feet. In worship and solitude–at peace with ourselves as we practice His presence and learn to wait and listen–*true love* will bear its fruit...leadership that can be trusted, filled with passion that is pure.

[1] Paraphrased overview of a section of *The Princess Bride*, 20th Century Fox Film Corp., 1987.

DISCUSSION PROBES:

1 Who in your ministry life has inspired you the most with his/her passion?
   - Name three ways he/she communicated that passion.
2. Have you ever tried to head up a project for which you had no personal passion?
   - What were the difficulties you encountered?
3. Have you ever become caught up in following someone whose passion was rooted in self-promotion?
   - What was the end result of his/her ministry?
   - What of lasting value was done?
   - What damage occurred?
4. Explain in your own words how to evaluate the source of someone's passion.
   - If you know the person well and sense wrong motives, how will you address the issue with them?
5. Develop a check list against which to test your own motives for getting involved in a project or ministry.
6. Describe your level of conviction of God's passion for you.
   - Under what circumstances have you doubted His love for you and what part do those doubts play in your ministry life now?
7. Give three reasons why the depth of your love for God is so critical as you walk in ministry and leadership.
8. Review the list of "Signs of Mixed Motives" on page 19. Discuss the dangers of each one.
   - Which, if any, are tendencies with which you personally struggle yourself?
9. Have you sought counsel with someone you trust who can help you pray through the pain of your life and bring healing and forgiveness to each troubling area?
   - If you haven't, will you commit to finding such a trusted person and begin the process?
10. Describe your day-to-day love relationship with God.
    - In what ways is the Holy Spirit working in your life to draw you to greater intimacy with Him?
    - How are you responding?

Chapter Two

FOLLOWING
THE FIRE

Trust in the Lord with all your heart and
lean not on your own understanding;
in all your ways acknowledge him,
and he will make your paths straight.
Proverbs 3:5, 6

God has, amazingly, chosen to change the world through us!
When He calls us—and fills our passion with His love,
opens doors and brings others alongside us who share our vision
and core values—nothing is impossible. Whether our mission glori-
fies Him or sinks into human error will depend upon our willingness to obey Him in all areas of our lives. This obedience will bring
humility, integrity and great influence—as well as His protection,
guidance, and the favor of men.

GOD'S WILL AND OUR MISSION

I once lived next door to a lovely young Christian woman who informed me one day that her calling was to be a great soloist. Rather than become involved in a local church and offer to serve and grow in discipleship in preparation for ministry, she spent her time at home practicing her singing, waiting to be discovered and promoted to the world. Of course, it never happened.

For too many of us, our concepts of vision and mission revolve around *us*, as though God creates plans to enhance our lives and give us importance.

However, I've discovered, as has Henry Blackaby, author of **Experiencing God**, that God's will is already in motion and revolves *not* around us, but around those who have not yet seen His glory or responded to His love. His vision is that the world be reconciled to Him at last; His plan is to heal the brokenhearted and set the captives free. As we worship Him and listen for His voice, He draws us into His plan to make the vision a reality. Any pursuit of ours that doesn't center upon making Him known isn't really ministry.

In searching for our mission, we should look around us. God somehow causes our gifts, our life experiences and our maturity to converge with a great need in the world or the church at just the right time! And then He brings others alongside us to launch the mission and see it through to victory.

ASKING THE RIGHT QUESTIONS

In discovering our part in His plan, there are definitely questions we can ask:

1. What is God's obvious desire for the people around me? What specific needs are surfacing?
2. How will my gifts, my season of life, my experience and my growth level play into meeting the specific need that is moving me with compassion?
3. Is what I believe God wants me to do being confirmed by the Holy Spirit—through the Word, other people (especially those

in authority over me), or by a witness within my own spirit?
Does filling this role make my heart "sing?"

4. Am I willing to pay the price required in time, energy and
personal sacrifice?

INTERRUPTED BY GOD

God has a disarming—and sometimes disconcerting—way of
interrupting our lives with an assignment that is key to His redemptive plan for mankind. Ten years prior to my call to raise up leaders,
God arrested me. While I was contentedly teaching, He stirred once
again the passion within me that I had tried to ignore—that of
addressing difficult issues in the ministry, including leadership gone
awry. He challenged me to give up teaching for a season to write
about them. In retrospect, what happened then reminded me of
watching Dr. Martin Luther King, Jr., back in the '60s, as he gave
his immortal speech, "I Have a Dream."

Just as Dr. King had seen the pain of his people who were victim-
ized by prejudice and bigotry—and were adding their own poison
to the melting pot—and wept for them, I began to weep for those in
ministry leadership whom I had seen wounded and wounding
others. My heart cried out to do something to make things different.
I saw clearly that people in ministry, through their sin and dishonoring of others, were breaking the heart of God. It was time to offer
relief, and he wanted to use me as part of His plan.

He gave me a vision of what life in the ministry could be like if
done *right*—if there were forgiveness and repentance and restoration, and if we would let the idol of "ministry" fall and worship God
alone. I hungered to see it come to pass and was suddenly ready to
pay whatever price would be required for my voice to be heard. I
realized at the time that God was calling me to bring whatever gifts
and skills I had to Him to be filled with His anointing so that His
dream of wholeness could be realized within the lives of those who
gave themselves daily for the cause of the Gospel.

Just as Dr. King did, I had a dream…a dream of ministry leadership done well that was so palpable to me that I could taste and
touch it with my eyes closed. I knew it was from God, and I knew

that I must give my life to pursue it. I had to stop all else and write about what I had seen, experienced and learned during my eighteen previous years in ministry. The purpose was to lovingly warn and encourage. We *had* to begin learning from our mistakes.

It necessitated surrendering my ministry position and salary at a time when we desperately needed the income. And how **Lambs on the Ledge** would become published, I didn't have a clue. Needless to say, during the two-and-one-half years it took to find the right publisher, my dream was repeatedly tested. If the dream had originated within my own heart alone, I would have given up. But since it was God's dream as well, I did not.

I realize *now* that before God could place me in a position of raising up the next generation of leaders, I needed to sort out what I had seen and experienced and be healed of my *own* wounds acquired during my years in serving under others. By finding the cross of Christ in repentance and forgiveness, and then being able to warn and encourage others—taking them back to the cross as well—God was preparing me to play my part in his plan to turn the tide in how leaders are developed in the ministry.

INTERRUPTED AGAIN

After settling into writing books and articles on issues of need in the church and ministry, God interrupted my plans again. While we were at our previous church, I was asked to give a leadership training seminar to the women leaders. This I willingly did because of the passion I have for leadership development, especially since it involved a one-time commitment of a few months. Such an interruption in the writing process wasn't that disturbing.

However, when my husband became the Church Administrator at New Life Church in Gahanna, Ohio, a year later and I was asked to be an Adult Intern in the Women's Ministries Department—which would quickly lead to becoming the Coordinator on staff—I balked badly. My first thought was that I had other priorities—a book to write, speaking engagements to honor and my own leadership training ministry to launch. Furthermore, I did not want to be pigeonholed in ministering to women *only*, after twenty years of

Following The Fire

ministering to both men and women. But God grabbed me by the ankles and wouldn't let me go. He also caused nearly every spring engagement to be mysteriously postponed until fall or later! One by one, my excuses evaporated.

After wrestling over the price to be paid in time, energy and commitment, I knew that God was asking me to move ahead in local leadership. One by one He dispelled my doubts and answered my questions about joining my passion and mission to those of the pastoral team. In fact, before I could even consider the position, I had to ask myself some responsible questions: Could I, indeed, buy into this church's vision? Did we share the same core values? Did my own purpose statement and giftings match or complement what they have been called to do? Could I continue to be myself and true to God's plan for my life while linking arms with this leadership team, without compromising something?

THE EFFICIENCY OF GOD

I quickly discovered the pastors' vision: To build a healthy church whose people are growing as disciples, doing the work of ministry and reaching the lost for Christ. I found that a very comprehensive discipleship and leadership training program was in place through which each new member passes. No church I had ever attended offered a better platform for leadership development! Here was a healthy organization within which I would be free to have a great impact in developing women for effective ministry and leadership.

My approach—a relational, heart-sensitive and healing one— would be a perfect complement to their goal and growth orientation. And, rather than having to address leaders after they have made all their mistakes, wounded others and been wounded— which had been much of my focus in the past—I would now have the joy of laying a firm foundation. This foundation would include creating an environment of integrity, of honoring others and of hunger for God that would engender godly, committed leaders. Then I began equipping, empowering, encouraging and releasing others—mentoring and coaching them to do the same to those in their own spheres of influence.

It became evident that the very issues about which I was currently writing in this book, I'd be able to live out. The principles I'd espoused would be tested in the fire of practical use. If they didn't work here, they'd not work anywhere. Conversely, if what I believed about raising up and releasing women to be world-changers *did* work here, this Women's Ministry would provide a model for other women's ministries all over the country!

When I finally surrendered and embraced God's purpose for my life during this season, His love for the men and women at New Life gripped my heart and drove me to my knees. I realized afresh that God was still passionate about the local church and has chosen her as His primary vehicle to reach out to the lost. As far as I was concerned, what was about to happen at New Life was all that mattered to God at this time, and He wanted it to matter to me as well.

I had much to learn. My call to the world would wait! His vision soon became my vision, and I embraced the call. He was at work among these precious people, preparing them for the great growth and harvest ahead. He had moved us to Ohio not only for Jim's job, but because I was to play a key role in bringing His will to pass through the Women's Ministries. What an honor!

INFLUENCING OTHERS

Whether we become teachers, writers, speakers, musicians, church planters, evangelists, children's or women's ministry leaders; whether we establish ministries to rescue the abused or addicted; or whether we respond to any number of other leadership challenges, others are watching us and will ultimately imitate us. As we learn in transparency and humility, others will learn from us. As is often said, "Leadership is caught, not taught."

For any ministry to endure, we must not only follow our calling in doing God's will, but must actively raise up and mentor well those whom He brings into our spheres of influence. As leaders, we are responsible to obey the mandate in II Timothy 2:2: *And the things you have heard me say in the presence of many witnesses entrust to reliable men who will also be qualified to teach others.*

Whatever we learn of Him, we are to pass on to others, bringing them also into the work of God. It is a great joy to use our influence to help others identify their places in the ministry of Jesus Christ, empowering them to do with excellence and great love all that God has asked them to do.

CONTAGIOUS ENERGY

Our vision and purpose define where we are going, how and what we will look like when we get there. As we blaze the trail, others catch the fire and vision, absorb the principles and apply the demonstrated strategies. Instead of plodding along behind us after we clear the brush away, our faith in them and God causes them to fan out beside us and level the ground, felling the trees on all sides. We move as one.

I have learned that, in a room of seven or more women, all the giftings needed to get a job done will be there. I have learned that women will rise to a challenge, respond with passion, and act with confidence against great odds—when the cause is just and the plan clear. I have further learned that trust, encouragement, grace and second chances produce leaders who continue to grow.

DEFINING OUR VISION AT NEW LIFE

As we asked God to show us His desire for the women at New Life Church, within the context of the church's overall passion for discipleship and evangelism, a clearly defined vision emerged. It is:

That all of us, regardless of age or life experience, become confident, healed and effective followers of Christ, influencing others to follow Him as well.

We then defined our Strategy:

- *To diligently pursue intimacy with God* through personal and corporate worship, Bible study and prayer.
- *To intentionally grow as believers* through participation in Life Groups, Discipleship Classes and Freedom Groups, mentoring and fellowship.

- *To continually learn and to deepen our commitments* through valuable seminars, conferences and retreats.
- *To joyfully serve others* by using our gifts and resources wisely and appropriately.
- *To lovingly reach out to our neighbors* with sincere friendship and a passion to introduce them to the Savior.

CORE BELIEFS

From the beginning of the process to the end, we kept clearly in mind our belief system:

1. *Women are loved and valued by God.*
2. *Women were created to reflect His glory and minister in His name.*
3. *Women who seek God and His ways influence others and turn hearts to Him.*
4. *Women's prayers move mountains.*

OUR RUDDER

Vision and purpose launch us, and passion fuels our progress, but what keeps us on course? What truly knits us to those who try to follow us and maintains "true north?"

Throughout our lives, whether we realize it or not, we are in the process of determining what is really important to us. As we mature, we find that what we value increasingly matches what is important to God. These core values steer our ministry and govern the way in which we carry out the mandates God places on our lives. Below are the core values that act as our rudder in the Women's Ministry at New Life Church:

1. *Authenticity.*
2. *Intimacy with God.*
3. *Healthy, honoring personal relationships.*
4. *A lifestyle of prayer and Spirit-led ministry to others.*

THE POWER OF SHARED VALUES

If the members of my leadership team—or the pastors and directors of New Life Church—did not share these values, we would be at sea as to how to minister together effectively, and with continuity. Without the energy of the unity that is generated by shared core values, we would be unable to sustain passion for any purpose over the long haul. Our ministry would be rife with inconsistencies in decision-making; direction would become fractured or confused; and we would all become disheartened, to say the least. We all must hold as precious the same concepts—beyond the obvious doctrinal tenets—for deep and lasting effectiveness.

For instance, if someone involved in New Life's Women's Ministry weren't authentic, she wouldn't dare get close enough to another woman in distress for fear her own weaknesses would be found out. Or if she didn't honor others, no one would be able to trust her leadership. If one of our leaders didn't value prayer, she would try to take the easiest route in a difficult situation, missing an opportunity to see what faith in God could do. All her expectations in pursuit of the vision would be limited by her human abilities.

BROAD SIGNIFICANCE

Dale E. Galloway, in the Nov./Dec. 2000 issue of *Net Results*, says that, "Without shared goal ownership, your ministry goes all over the place—everywhere and nowhere." The same hold true for shared values. As we serve together, we must care about the same things and have the same indisputable convictions. Otherwise, there will be no sound and understandable basis for making decisions or taking action.

Aubrey Malphurs, in his book *Values-Driven Leadership*, says that core values will:

1. Determine Ministry Distinctives. (They draw a clear picture of what we are about.)
2. Dictate Personal Involvement. (They are capable of drawing passionate responses from those who share them.)
3. Communicate What Is Important. (Whenever a decision is to

be made, they point us in a constant and consistent direction.)

4. Embrace Positive Change. (They should be able to grow and reflect the intensified work of God in our midst.)

5. Influence Overall Behavior. (Guide in making decisions and responding to changes.)

6. Inspire People to Action. (They are a powerful rallying point.)

7. Enhance Credible Leadership. (They clearly show that the leader knows the mandate on the ministry and is committed to pursue it.)

8. Shape Ministry Character. (Everything we do will reflect where our heart is.)

9. Contribute to Ministry Success. (They keep us focused and forward moving.)

NEVER A DULL MOMENT

At just the moment we think we have mastered something, God plunges us into a new learning experience! Rarely does our calling remain in a static context; God's development of the leader within us requires movement from one challenge to another, often in very different settings. Growth requires new crises of belief, fresh testing and stretching of our abilities, new situations where our theories are required to become action and our weakest leadership muscles exercised.

We must be ready to move with God when the cloud and the fire move. We must be willing to go and do whatever He dictates, however obscure or however intimidating, whether it seems beneath us or far beyond our abilities. God knows what experiences are needed to train us and to refine the passion that burns in our bones, so that it will not scorch the earth or leave those around us dry and dusty. Once we begin our apprenticeship under Him—irresistibly drawn by the will of God that has captured our hearts—there is no turning back. What matters to Him, increasingly matters to us, and is forever inescapable.

So let's buckle our seatbelts and commit ourselves to the journey! May we obey with humility and move with grace, remembering always that to carry His name and struggle for His cause are the highest honors on earth.

DISCUSSION PROBES:

1. What preparation or additional training should you be pursuing to enhance your effectiveness as a leader?
2. How do you guard your heart against the temptation to promote yourself in an effort to get into, or increase your influence in, ministry?
3. Carefully and honestly answer the questions posed on p. 26-27, "Asking the Right Questions."
4. Describe the latest experience you have had of being interrupted by God to act on a pressing need. What character quality did it devlop within your life to obey Him at that time? How has it enhanced your leadership ability?
5. Have you been held up because of wounds and fears you still carry? Determine now to seek counseling for them. Healing will involve releasing resentment and unfulfilled expectations; repenting of your judgments and forgiving.
6. What is the vision and mission of your ministry or the ministry with which you are associated? Do they match what is in your heart?
7. If you don't train and equip those under you, what will happen when you delegate an area to them?
8. As you look at the church and the world, what issues make you weep? Is God asking you to prepare to make a difference?
9. Explain "Leadership is caught, not taught." What are those around you "catching" from your example?
10. What are your personal core values—the values that reflect the underlying convictions that guide you in making decisions personally and in the ministry?

Chapter Three

A HEART THAT HONORS

Do nothing out of selfish ambition or vain conceit,
but in humility consider others better than yourselves.
Philippians 2:15

Calvin Miller, in his book, *The Singer*, says that love often stands quite close to hate "...like silent chessmen, side by side. Only the color of the squares is different." In one moment, we can be loving and honoring, and in the next, hating and dishonoring! Unfortunately, it's true.

We all know that we're commanded to love God and one another—that there will be no blessing if we hate. Yet we cross the fine line between these two extremes in a heartbeat. Whenever we diminish, dismiss, disregard or despise another's life—*including our own*—we move from one square on the chessboard to another, reversing the color of the squares upon which our hearts rest. If we remain there, the game may be lost.

It doesn't matter whether the dishonoring is toward those in authority over us or toward those under our own authority, or even a neglect of ourselves and our need for boundaries and respect. The principles are the same. Valuing is at the heart of love. If we are not willing to value and honor, we will never love, no matter how hard we try.

HONORING OTHERS

Honoring is the starting point for every leader who desires to please God and be effective. If we value others by attaching high worth to their lives—regardless of their behavior at any given moment—we will not slander, despise, wound or neglect them. We will see them as individually precious to God, and therefore individually precious to us.

We will remember well the weaknesses in *our own* lives, and will therefore find patience for the same in theirs. But, because we love them, we won't want to leave them where they are. We will long for them to share the freedom we have found in trusting God as we honor others.

We must dream—dream of their success and begin to invest in our relationships with them. Because we recognize their great worth to God—after all, He sent His beloved Son to *die* for them— we will have the courage to gently urge them to reconsider their choices as well as affirm their progress. But this can be done only after their trust has been earned by our own faithfulness to them.

HONORING AUTHORITIES

There is a vast difference between grieving over a wrong, making an appeal for change and then trusting God within how they choose to respond and, on the other hand, condemning and spreading our chagrin to others. We must remember that only God is the judge of the world. When we play judge, jury and hangman of another, we are on dangerous ground—ground in which blooms the noxious weeds of arrogance and self-righteous rebellion.

David, of biblical fame, knew this. He was amazing! He actually *loved* the man who used him for target practice! He remembered Saul's greatness and looked only at his tortured heart—and grieved for him. How could he manage to love this man who relentlessly sought to kill him?

Very simply, he honored Saul...*because he honored God*. David must have had a very astute comprehension of the seriousness of the order of authority God had established through the prophet's anointed choice of king. While that man sat on the throne, respecting the king's authority and personhood superseded every other logical design on earth. Every action of David's—from sparing Saul's life in the cave and again on the field while Saul lay sleeping, to appealing to the king's memory of their years together and his own faithfulness—showed how highly he valued and loved this mad king.

Finally, Saul was defeated in battle and fell upon his own sword. When an Amalekite finished the job and delivered the news of Saul's death, David's troops were overjoyed! At last, David could take his place on the throne and bring the nation together and restore sanity to kingship.

But what was David's response in hearing the news? He tore his clothes, mourned, wept and fasted until evening for Saul, Jonathan and the slain of the army of Israel, the very army that had pursued him all those years. (He even had the Amalekite killed who had run the nearly-dead Saul through at Saul's request!)

Furthermore, he composed a lament to honor the slain king and his son and ordered all of Judah to sorrow and sing it with him. The lament, instead of recounting all of Saul's weaknesses, recounted Saul's glory and strength. David honored his enemy even in death. (II Samuel 1)

HONORING THOSE UNDER OUR AUTHORITY

Honoring our followers is as important as honoring our authorities, and I love the way Jesus honored His followers. He never reminded them of their shady pasts, their lack of education, the blunders they made while learning how to trust God—not even their betrayal and abandonment of him in his greatest hour of need.

Instead, He attached high worth to them. He confided in them; patiently explained spiritual truths in terms they could understand; and listened to them even when they were being petty. He made sure their basic physical needs were being met; prayed for them; and shared His glory with them. Furthermore, Jesus looked beyond their gender and economic status and into their hearts; expected the best from them; made great promises to them that He kept; and comforted them and loved them to the death. Even after He had seemingly left them at the cross, He reappeared to encourage them and to instruct them on how to carry on in the power of the Holy Spirit whom He would send in His absence. The way in which He passed the task onto his future leaders was flawless! And with His blessing and anointing upon them, they turned the world upside down.

We are here as believers today because of the way in which He honored these men and women every step of the way. Never did He mock or ridicule them, devalue or distrust them, even in their failures and weakness. He knew they would learn, and that learning would take time. He lovingly invested that time. He honored and valued them...and they knew it. In response, they were willing to give up everything to follow Him!

And through it all, just as David honored Jehovah, Jesus honored His Father. If David and Jesus had not honored God's method, system and plan, they would have failed as leaders. We, like they, will succeed as leaders only if we honor and respect in both directions—God and those going before us as leaders, and those coming after us in whom we are responsible to invest our lives.

THROUGH OUR UNIQUE STRENGTHS

God has equipped us as women with many unique strengths that are needed for effective leadership. When we honor, we are textbook examples of good leadership! But when we forget to honor—when we don't respect our authorities, when we don't value ourselves enough to say "no" or stop others from abusing us, or when we treat others as expendable tools for our own promotion—we cross the line to hate. It is all downhill from there.

I believe that one reason men sometimes have such a hard time welcoming us as co-laborers is that they have too often seen our dishonoring behavior and have thought that to be an accurate picture of who we inevitably will be at all times. Many have written us off because of the weaknesses they have seen. But—for the sake of the Body of Christ—and the future authenticity of the Christian message—I pray that they will increasingly make the effort to understand us and give us a chance to rise to God's call within honoring. May we not disappoint them.

HOW WE HONOR VS. DISHONOR

THROUGH OUR NATURAL STRENGTHS

Nurturing

Mentor others	vs	Create dependence and a following
Equip, train and promote		Manipulate for control
Encourage and correct gently		Play favorites

Consensus Building

Gather info from others		Manipulate info— means to an end
Connect people with the info	vs	Lose our focus a midst the issues
Invite ideas and creativity		Complicate the goal
Adapt easily; Delegate		Develop exclusive circles

Communicative

Cast vision with great passion		Talk much more than listen
Keep our word; Say		Must have the last word
what we mean	vs	
Rally others		Betray confidences
Give voice to others' concerns		Overstate and give too many details
Create and maintain a sense of community		Triangulate issues

Spiritually Sensitive

Understand God's embrace in solitude		Run on past experiences with God
Love to worship	vs.	Neglect the Word and prayer
Sense His direction		Won't slow down to listen to Him
Reflect His character		Spiritually arrogant; condemn others

Ready to Serve

Quick to volunteer		Let others take advantage of us
Faithful in obscurity	vs.	Get comfortable and resist change
Act without promise of reward		Think ourselves incapable of leading when God calls us to do so

Compassionate

In touch with real issues		Kill ourselves trying to be heroes
Willing to feel others' pain	vs.	Use ministry for emotional compensation
Will sacrifice to help the wounded		Neglect our families for a cause and prevent abuse

Intuitive About Evil

Keen judge of character   vs   Judge others while unwilling to see our own sin

Able to discern the roots of sin   Above correction when we're wrong

Submit to authorities when principles Are understood   Placate by passivity rather than appeal Demean authorities to others

Fearless For a Cause

Willing to risk danger or defeat Full of passion   vs   Apt to run ahead of God Refuse counsel and accountability

Willing to face impossible odds   Bend the rules to achieve a goal

Highly Relational

Foster interdependence and cooperation   vs   Get caught up emotionally in harmful relationships

Sensitive when addressing a problem or conflict   Deceived by affirmation; perform for approval

Value relationships over functions   Use relationships to get our way

Able to identify with others deeply   Easily offended by remarks or actions of others

Will laugh and cry with others   Remember forever wrongs done to us

Persevering

Learn from the defeats		Persist after the Holy Spirit has ceased to anoint our efforts
Willing to try another approach	vs	Ignore warning signs of danger
		Push our people beyond reason
Will stay in until the goal is reached		Arrogant; unwilling to repent and stop
		Bitter in failure

Multi-Tasked

Pursue many projects at once without losing focus		Neglect solitude with God
Consider ramifications as well as actions	vs	Impatient with others
Resourceful; will empower others		Become over-extended

Peace Making

Use conflict constructively to bring growth		Practice avoidance, compensation, triangulation or manipulation rather than confront
	vs	
Long to see people reconciled		Try to fix everyone
Quick to repent and forgive		Hold grudges

FINDING THE CROSS

We will not always do it right. When spears are thrown at us, we may pull one or two right out of the wall and heave them back; or when we are betrayed by someone into whose life we have poured our own, we may bitterly denigrate him or her to our friends.

But when we do, we must return to the cross, learning to quickly repent of playing God in our attempt to make them pay for what Jesus has already died. When we forgive, God will lovingly extract the sin lodged in our hearts and bring healing for our own wounds. If we have spoken bitter words to them, heartfelt apologies must be made and honoring renewed within us.

If we have fallen into the trap of thinking *we* are the center of the ministry and have become dictatorial, surrounding ourselves with "yes men" and resorting to harmful methods to retain power and keep "our" ministries going, God will draw us up short. He will be the "hound of heaven," pursuing us with conviction until we humble ourselves at His feet.

We *will* find our way to the cross—the most important path we will travel in life, and one that we will travel time and time again. When we sin, the joy of repenting and giving the rule of the world back to God, and the delight of being washed clean as we forgive, will never grow old. When we repent, honoring is reestablished as Jesus reassures us of His love, clears our vision and sets us right again.

But how much better it would be *not* to sin! If we will daily pray this prayer of David's as recorded in Ps. 139:23-24, "Search me, O God, and know my heart; test me and know my anxious thoughts. See if there is any offensive way in me, and lead me in the way everlasting," He will show us our weaknesses and give us grace to love and lead unselfishly. In His presence in worship and prayer, we will experience His humility, and *His* leadership will take root in our hearts. Even when we feel unqualified and have doubts about ourselves, he will give us the grace to complete the mission before us.

THE POWER OF HONORING

Meanwhile, we must honor and love sincerely. By valuing others before God, truth can be spoken, even in correction. As we are considerate—not demanding servitude from others—the climate changes and they are freed to serve out of the same love that we have demonstrated. *We must be what we want them to be!* They will learn by watching and interrelating with us. How we want our ministry to be at its best, we must establish from the beginning.

Nurturing and encouraging, as well as empowering and releasing, will become the lifestyle of our ministry or organization—if it is first our own lifestyle. As we take delight in our people, they will learn to dream, and the dreams will connect them to great missions God has for them. We will soon experience the amazing joy of seeing them soar in ministry beyond where we have gone.

This is our goal as leaders: To connect others to the Lord and His plan for them by ministering to them in a way that is honoring. Godly results are obtained no other way!

DISCUSSION PROBES:

1. Study Matt. 5-7 and list the ways Jesus teaches us to honor others.
   - Which are the hardest for you? Why?
2. In what ways do you see other leaders devaluing themselves?
   - Are you guilty of any of the same patterns? If so, which ones?
   - Describe how these patterns impede your leading freely and effectively.
3. Picture before you the primary authority in your own life or ministry. How do you feel in your heart toward him/her?
   - Do you truly want your authority to be highly successful?
   - How would you respond if your diligence in serving them brought no gratitude or recognition from them?
   - What steps could you take in keeping your spirit free from resentment or bitterness, or your heart from closing down?
4. What are the components of making a godly appeal to authority for change?
   - What parts do forgiveness and release of expectations play?
5. In which ways do you identify with how Jesus honored His followers as described in this chapter?
   - Are you being convicted of unloving behavior or attitudes toward one or more of your followers, co-workers or employees? If so, stop now and ask God's forgiveness. Ask the Holy Spirit to reveal to you how Jesus sees them and to begin changing your heart.
6. Using a scripture passage of your choice, describe how honoring others is rooted in honoring God.
7. Explore the HONOR VS. DISHONOR Chart on p. 42-45. Star the aspects of honoring that come most easily for you.
   - Highlight the aspects of dishonoring with which you struggle.
8. Ask God to reveal to you the root cause of dishonoring of yourself, God or others.
   - Journal in a notebook the insights you receive and any break-throughs that occur as you submit each weakness to Him.

9. Take any steps that are immediately possible to change behavior that has been unknowingly dishonoring. When necessary, ask forgiveness of someone you have dishonored or disregarded.
10. Ask a trusted co-worker to hold you accountable for change.

Chapter Four

THE MATURING OF OUR GIFTS

*For this reason I remind you
to fan into flame the gift of God...
For God did not give us a spirit of timidity,
but a spirit of power,
of love and of self-discipline.*
II Timothy 1:6, 7

We are each "a work in progress." As we obey God in serving others, He stretches us, changes us and brings greater depth and balance to our giftings.

When I took the Spiritual Gifts Test for the first time about twenty years ago, I scored high in exhortation, teaching and mercy, but low in leadership, prophecy and giving. But as God took me on an interesting journey into leadership, I had to stretch to embrace the skills required to do each job. While responding creatively to the tremendous need in those around me in the ministry, and through God dealing with my heart through the years, He has amazed me by His awesome grace in capacitating me to do things for which I felt unprepared.

RESPONDING TO A NEED

When I began teaching at Teen Challenge Training Center back in 1974, my vision and passion were to see former addicts and alcoholics discipled and walking in maturity with God. However, it wasn't long before I noticed that, occasionally, very sincere students dropped out early in the program for no apparent reason. After watching them closely, I discovered a common thread running through these cases...the thread of illiteracy. I felt strongly that something had to be done about it. While my authorities recognized the problem, none felt compelled to meet the need at that time. However, they encouraged me to do whatever I could and provided the classroom for it.

I had neither previous interest nor training in teaching someone to read, but I set out to learn. Through an area elementary school I was able to get out-of-date reading books and old, half-used workbooks free. One by one, on my own time, I began teaching these men how to read.

After several months, I heard that the state offered grants to local agencies to fund Adult Basic Education classes. I wrote a proposal, including my objectives and an assessment of the materials and equipment I would need, and submitted it through the local community college. I was awarded the grant and began to build a remedial reading program that could serve all the men at Teen Challenge who were functioning below a fifth grade reading level.

DEALING WITH GROWTH

I soon had more students than I could handle alone. I needed to recruit and train assistant teachers. After getting the permission of the Teen Challenge Program Director, I began my search among the student body. I carefully watched the academically gifted students in my second-month English class who demonstrated an honest concern for struggling fellow students. I looked for men with a solid relationship with God who were: willing to learn, honest, good communicators, patient, dependable and self-disciplined. I then taught them what I had learned. These men then became my staff team.

With the help of eight or nine assistant teachers at any given time—and some creative scheduling—we were able to effectively teach nearly forty men per year, one-on-one, as well as tutor them in the mainstream class material during their 9 or 10 months in the program. Many of the remedial students even earned their Graduate Equivalency Diplomas!

I eventually supplemented the individual instruction with computerized, Bible-based literacy material developed and supplied by Project Light out of Virginia Beach, VA. Using computers not only made learning easier for the visual and tactile learners, it also introduced all the men to basic computer skills.

After lobbying the Center Vocational Director for many months to declare the Remedial Reading Room a vocational trade area, we were granted equal status among the many other trade training areas at the Center. From then on, my assistant teachers were rewarded at their own graduations with vocational teaching certificates issued by Teen Challenge.

During the first few years, as enrollment in the remedial program grew and I added more and more assistant teachers, my administrative duties multiplied as well. I was soon the department head, overseeing all functions of a diverse department. I found myself involved more in training teachers and giving spiritual leadership to my teaching team than directly teaching remedial students. Without noticing, I had become a leader and a trainer of leaders.

AMAZING RESULTS

As the leader of that department, I was blessed beyond measure to see my original vision fulfilled. As the remedial students painstakingly mastered the art of reading and writing and successfully remained in the Teen Challenge program, they were able to be discipled in the Word and mature in Christ.

But my joy multiplied as I watched my assistant teachers blossom. They grew in confidence in their giftings; increased in their sensitivity to the struggles of others and their ability to see complex "people projects" through to the end; learned to delight in seeing others succeed; mastered working as a team and deepened their relationships with God. They came to love one another and formed friendships that will last a lifetime. Furthermore, many of these teachers were inspired to go on to college and pursue teaching careers because of their experiences as assistant remedial teachers.

I discovered through this process that *effective leadership is not about power or control, but about creating an environment for success and developing the God-given potential in those under my immediate care.* In turn, they simply emulated this pattern with their charges and brought about the fulfillment not only of our shared vision, but that of the many to whom they ministered. We all grew as we responded to the challenge, and we accomplished as a team many times over what we ever could have accomplished individually.

THE STEPS I USE TODAY
AS A RESULT OF THIS EXPERIENCE

1. Recognize the need and cast vision
2. Pray with prayer partners and watch as God brings like-impassioned team players to me
3. Set goals and develop a strategy
4. Submit plans to my authorities or people who can advise me and hold me accountable
5. Seek God for the resources; think creatively regarding needs
6. Sacrifice to make a difference
7. Build and equip the team members, mentoring them and encouraging them to improve on my methods
8. Model responsible behavior and spiritual discipline
9. Build unity and team spirit
10. Celebrate the wins
11. Evaluate the losses and learn from them
12. Give glory to God for the results

A SHIFT IN GIFTING

When I took the same Spiritual Gifts Test after developing the remedial reading department, I was amazed by the shift in my scores. They were highest in *leadership* and then exhortation, followed closely by prophecy, which had grown because of my need as a leader to be discerning. Teaching followed as a tight fourth. As I had matured and been obedient to the vision God had given me for challenging the illiteracy barrier at Teen Challenge so that the men could succeed in the program, my gifts had matured as well. Because of my passion for the vision, I had simply exercised the necessary gifts which then were forced to grow in strength.

I learned from the experience that our gifts are not static and that we can't simply opt out of a challenge by saying, "That's not my gift." We must be continually growing and maturing. While one gift may consistently dominate, God will stretch other gifts whenever they are needed to fulfill the visions God has given us.

CONVERGENCE IN GIFTING

Not long ago, I took the Spiritual Gifts Tests for the third time. I was startled to find that all the gifts registered within 2 points of each other, with only giving lower than the rest. (I have since asked the Lord for a giving heart—one that takes joy in meeting others' physical and material needs. I am taking advantage of opportunities to grow in this area.) J. Robert Clinton, author of **The Making of a Leader**, explains the equalizing of our gifts as the convergence that occurs as one becomes more mature. That's exciting! Evidently, as we synthesize all the lessons and experiences we have had through life, we find that we have been broadened and trained by them in many ways. Wisdom is on the horizon. Finally!

Mr. Clinton defines the first phase of the process "Sovereign Foundations," when God works through our families or our environment to teach us to respond positively to challenges and take advantage of what He has sown into our lives. The second phase is

"Inner-Life Growth," in which God uses testing experiences to develop character within us, and our leadership potential is identified. Phase III, "Ministry Maturing," follows. This is when we as leaders begin reaching out to others. We are identifying our spiritual gifts and coming to understand how our ministry can be useful within the larger context of the Body of Christ.

Clinton says that, "Ministry activity or fruitfulness is not the focus of Phases I, II, and III. God is working primarily in the leader, not through him or her."[2]

In Phase IV, "Life Maturing," the leader is coming to truly know God by first-hand experience, and his or her ministry is bearing good fruit. The key to development during this phase is "...a positive response to the experiences God ordains. This response will deepen communion with God that will become the base for lasting and effective ministry."[3]

Then comes V, "Convergence"—when ministry is maximized. We learn during this stage where we can have the greatest effectiveness and we learn how to say "no" to those activities at which we are not the best. We are also learning how to trust, rest and watch as God moves us into place.

According to Clinton, the final phase will be "Afterglow," or "Celebration," when the "...fruit of a lifetime of ministry and growth culminates in an era of recognition and indirect influence at broad levels. Others will seek them out because of their consistent track record in following God. There will be no recognizable developmental task other than to allow a lifetime of ministry to reflect the glory of God..."[4]

GRACE

If, right now, we feel totally inadequate for the missions facing us, we are in a good place. Inadequacy drives us to our knees where we are enabled to rediscover grace–that supernatural ability to do the naturally impossible. It is a marvel how God graces us when we are well aware of our weaknesses—but are willing to risk and learn from Him and others. He covers even our mistakes with His grace, and through them teaches us the greatest of leadership lessons.

Nothing is lost or wasted when we embrace our experiences gratefully and are merely humble and obedient. That's all He asks.

[2] Dr. J. Robert Clinton, *The Making of a Leader*, p. 45.

[3] Ibid.

[4] Ibid, p. 46

DISCUSSION PROBES:

1. Take a Spiritual Gifts Test. Were there any surprises as to your strengths or weaknesses?
   - List your 3 strongest and your 3 weakest.
2. If you have taken a Spiritual Gifts Test previously, compare the results.
   - What has changed?
   - Connect the changes with events in your life that forced the growth to occur.
3. If you have had an experience of spearheading or developing a new project, define the steps you took to reach your goal and fulfill your vision.
4. Define in your own words what it means to equip and empower others to do a task.
   - Do you characteristically equip and empower others to get the job done, or do you attempt to remain the central figure in each step of development?
5. Describe your attitude, as a leader, toward co-workers when your vision includes their success and fulfillment in ministry.
6. Describe a great lesson your have learned either through:
   - Micromanaging a project
   - empowering and trusting others to follow through on their own.
7. Discuss the Steps on p. 54 and their importance to a ministry.
   - Which step do you typically omit or pursue inadequately?
   - What problems develop as a result?
8. Within which period of life, according to Clinton, are you now?
9. Have you ever turned down a task without praying about it first, offering the reason as, "That's not my gift?'
   - How has your thinking changed as a result of studying this chapter?
10. Take time now to journal a prayer to God confessing mistakes He has revealed to you during this session.
    - Thank Him for forgiving you and giving you new opportunities to serve Him more effectively.
    - Commit yourself to be a student of good leadership.

Section Two:

BUILDING A STRONG FOUNDATION

Chapter Five

SHARING INFLUENCE

From him, the whole body, joined and held together
by every supporting ligament,
grows and builds itself up in love,
as each part does its work.
Ephesians 4:16

As the last woman disappeared through the fellowship hall door and out into the night, Melody slumped into a chair and laid her aching head on the brightly colored tablecloth draped over the table beside her. The women's event had been a huge success, but no one had remained to celebrate it with her. She had put it together alone, had carried it off alone, and now was alone to clean up.

"I guess I'm not the great leader I thought I was. I haven't the stamina for this!" she whispered to herself in despair.

Just then, Pastor Wilson unexpectedly poked his head through the door. "Need some help, Melody?" he asked with a smile.

Gratefully, she lifted her weary head and nodded assent.

As they filled the last two trash bags and set them by the back door, her pastor asked softly, "Why didn't you get help for this event? Delegation is a wonderful invention, you know!"

"Well," faltered Melody as she straightened her back and brushed a wayward strand of blond hair from her eyes, "I didn't know whom to ask. When I inherited the position of Women's Ministry leader, everyone just looked at me with relief and said I'd do a great job. No one volunteered to help me," she answered with a sigh.

"Could it be that they need to learn about teamwork?" he probed gently as they headed toward the coat rack in the foyer.

"But where do I start? I've never built a team before. I'm just a housewife with a vision for women reaching women for Christ," Melody answered with intensity mixed with frustration. "It seems that there is an army of untapped potential within the women of this church, but I'm tired of having teas and craft nights. I want to see our neighbors saved and our women grow into spiritual maturity. I want those who have been abused healed, and broken marriages restored!" Melody's passion was clear and she was becoming more animated with every word. She was speaking what she could clearly "see" in the spirit. It was a vision that burned in her bones.

"I thought that if I had a big event that allowed the women to begin to open up to each other, they would catch the vision and want to be a part of it," she concluded with obvious disappointment.

Pastor Wilson rubbed his chin thoughtfully. "Well, your vision is in line with the mission of this church and your heart and life are submitted to God, so I believe He has chosen you for the task." He paused, then continued slowly, "But have you ever *defined* your vision in simple terms that everyone could grasp? Maybe you could start there."

"I guess I haven't made it very clear," she faltered. "I'll do that, but then what?" Melody queried. "How do I find the key people and get them involved?"

His eyes sparkled as a plan began to take shape in his mind. "How about starting with a night of prayer once every two weeks for all who have a burden for women's ministry. I'll give you pulpit time beforehand to share your vision and invite all who want to know more." Pastor Wilson was becoming excited. "Then," he continued, "out of that group watch for 4 or 5 who are most faithful.

Begin meeting with them individually, getting to know them, their backgrounds and their spiritual gifts. Let them get to know you as well. *Be transparent yourself, so they can begin to trust you,"* he emphasized. "After a few months, call them together and help them share with each other. And don't rush. This isn't a race!" he chuckled. "Get it as right as you can from the beginning."

"What kind of gifts should I look for in these women?" Melody asked, fascinated by this simple plan.

"Look at Moses," he answered thoughtfully. "He was burning himself out. He needed Aaron as an executive liaison to help spread his vision; he needed Jethro to advise him and hold him accountable; he needed Joshua and Caleb who would work in the trenches with commitment and integrity. He needed Miriam to encourage him and priests to pray for him."

Melody was getting the picture, all kinds of ideas and possibilities spinning through her mind, but still wondering if she could make it happen.

"And you can call me anytime you need advice," he reassured her. "I'm here to help you succeed, and I mean that," he stated emphatically.

Just as they reached the front door, her husband Greg pulled up at the curb to pick Melody up. The pastor waved at him and shouted a greeting, and then headed to his own car and home.

As she slid into the front seat, Greg asked gently, "So how did it go?"

"Great!" she smiled with obvious relief. "It's a fresh beginning. I'm going to build a team!"

A NEW DAY

Gone are the days of the Lone Ranger and the Superstar. We have finally shed the illusion that a leader is the solitary hero who fights the world's battles single-handedly. In fact, few people trust that kind of leader anymore. It is too dangerous for the followers…and too lonely for the leader.

The church is called a body for a very good reason; each part needs all the others and none can sustain the life of the body alone.

We can be set free by sharing our influence with others through teamwork. Best of all, as we learn how to complement one another, those who share our passion and want to move with us in God's plan will do so with one mind and heart.

RECKONING FIRST WITH THE PAST

Sometimes we are asked to lead a ministry that has had no formal structure and we are free to make a fresh start, just as was Melody. Occasionally, we are able to pick up right where the previous leader left off—especially if we were mentored within that ministry. If changes need to be made, these changes can be eased into place as we focus our attention on what is most effective.

At other times, however, we inherit a previous leader's team and mission, neither of which suits what God has asked us to do. It takes enormous courage, but we must build our own team and cast fresh vision born of the current spiritual, emotional or physical needs of those to whom we are called to minister. This holds true whether we are a church or para-church leader.

It is very difficult to effect a new ministry plan while there are still people attached to the old; new wine needs a new wineskin. As time-devouring as it will be, the old program or paradigm must be allowed to go through a death before the new can come. While this is occurring, we will have the opportunity to affirm the former leaders and the ministry that is ending. Those who have led in the past *deserve* honor and gratitude. As we will soon learn, leading a ministry is no easy task! They need our applause for all their sacrifice and accomplishments, and we need to give it in order to appreciate into what we ourselves are walking as we take up the reins. A bridge of appreciation for the past–and how it has led us to the present–must be built or seeds of resentment could fester within those still planted on the receding bank.

That the former methods and strategies often must be retired is natural and not be construed as anyone's fault–especially not ours. If we have been appointed or elected and our vision has our board of directors' or church leadership's blessing, we can go through the disconcerting death throes without guilt. We may have to weather misunderstandings and criticism while the old is phased out and a clean slate prepared, but if we have given honor and thanks to those who have preceded us, celebrating their wins, the air will clear more quickly. While it is clearing, we can lovingly assure them that all will be well in time.

If we hold to our vision, stay on our knees in prayer, love generously and remember that the call to set fresh direction has come from God Himself, we will be able to remain sweet in spirit. Eventually the old will have been laid to rest and they will be ready to embrace the new.

MEANWHILE

We can learn a lot about the culture of our organization or church by spending time with the preceding generation of leaders. We should visit them armed with questions, and be ready to just sit and listen. They will likely have invaluable advice for us. As we spend time with them we may, in fact, find one with whom we quickly relate and whom we will want to ask to mentor us for a season.

We must also get to know the younger generation and those who may be new to our body or staff. A few of the questions for which we will seek answers are:

1. What are their felt needs?
2. What experiences do they bring with them?
3. What are their spiritual gifts?
4. How can we help them in their relationship with Christ and their growth as believers in the world?
5. If they could design the ministry, what would it look like?

As we get a consensus of what they are looking for, we will be able to identify the specific purposes of the ministry. We can listen to new ideas; they may be better than our own! Later, after forming our leadership team, we will use this information, in discussion with our teammates, to clarify the vision and help craft our mission statement.

TRUST GROWS

As we listen to others and share the emerging vision one-on-one with others, keeping it simple and clear, their trust in our motives will grow and word will spread that our vision is worthy. Before long, a new expectancy will burgeon, and as the old is laid to rest, everyone will be ready to go on in a new direction.

Ultimately, we will be only as effective as leaders as we are clear about what we believe God is commissioning us to do together. *The more consistently and clearly we share the vision, the greater will be the energy it will command when launched.* Spending time with others and letting them know our hearts will also pay great dividends when the time comes to pull together our team players. Trust will have been built, and respect for our choice of teammates will follow.

As the vision catches fire in *their* hearts, we need to find their individual passions and encourage them to dream big within their areas of giftings and expertise. People long to make a significant difference with their lives and desperately need to be challenged and energized to take action. As we help them prepare, God will guide us to others who are needed to complete the dream. In fact, I have discovered that anytime an authentic need—one that God wants our ministry to address—becomes apparent, God will have already put in place those gifted and passionate to do something about that need. *God* supplies. We merely *pay attention* to what He is doing and concentrate on developing the people around us.

ESTABLISHING TEAMS

In some situations, we inherit employees or elected officials who are automatically part of our leadership team. Other short-term teams will be formed from time to time, drawn from the ministry at large, when needed for problem-solving or to perform a specified task. But boards and directors will likely be there for the duration. Our greatest challenge will be to involve them deeply in leadership rather than leaving them to be merely observers who critique us.

However, while we draw in ideas and build consensus, we must remember to keep final authority within our own hands for the sake of the mission. We are ultimately responsible for its outcome. If we are wise, our policy regarding who receives the credit or blame will be: If the mission fails, *we* as the leaders take the blame; but if it succeeds, we give *our team members* the credit.

If we can choose the members of our council or board, we must do so based on *shared core values, compassion, character and gifting*–not on their charisma, popularity or visibility. Even if they are inexperienced in ministry but are teachable, we have discovered a gold mine of potential. Mentoring them will bring these prospective leaders up to speed before long.

A word of caution: We must be careful, however, not to assign positions with titles before we mentor someone inexperienced. It is very difficult to reverse such an action should the novice prove to be a poor fit or lack the commitment needed. Premature elevation is a setup for later frustration for everyone. (See **Lambs on the Ledge** for a discussion of favoritism and premature elevation.)

RESIST MICRO-MANAGING

Once we release areas of responsibility to members of our leadership team, or to any of the short-term teams, we must resist monitoring every move and decision they make. We will, of course, be there to give counsel and to cheer them on. However, we must trust them and support them, giving them space to test their own wings, *whether they succeed or fail.*

In fact, failures are most often followed by new ideas and creativity, and are not to be feared. Indeed, the best lessons are learned through failure. We can then come alongside them and help them "fail forward," as leadership guru John Maxwell often says. Together, we can ask, "What would Jesus do to turn this around?" Their personal restoration and reinstatement, if possible, are more important than any project. Much is learned in failure: humility, grace, the ability to assess and make adjustments, gratitude for counsel, to name a few. When the dust settles, they will be wiser and will know how to likewise empower others, exhibiting the same trust we have given them.

Continually, we must let people know that we believe in them.

In the end, no matter what is endured in the process of growth, they will rise to what we believe about them. And because attitudes are contagious, our positive, constructive approach will cause others to adapt to our example. Conversely, if we appear irritated about the challenges we face, then our team members will become irritated and discouraged, fear failure and lose hope. Then no one grows.

CELEBRATE

At intervals along the way, we must show our appreciation to those who have stepped up to the plate to learn from us how to minister effectively. As Coordinator of the Women's Ministries at my church, I give a catered pool party each summer for all the ladies who have been involved in any way in Women's Ministry—whether in putting together our "Big Events" or Spring Retreat, coaching, or leading or apprenticing in one of our small groups. I've arranged this to say "Thank you" to them for their faithfulness and to celebrate the victories of this year. Not only will they know that I value them, but they will bond with each other, unconsciously being strengthened in their commitments to the Lord, the mission and one another.

BENEFITS OF TEAM MINISTRY

Building teams can be a challenge, but the end result is worth it all. Some of the benefits are:

1. More complete ministry will be provided as more gifts are employed.
2. New ideas will emerge providing diversity and variety.
3. Members will learn to trust, communicate honestly and submit to one another.
4. There will be accountability as our lives and motives are open to teammates' loving input.
5. When everyone shares responsibility for success, all will make a deep investment in the vision and mission.
6. Team members will experience empowerment as leadership

shifts to them when their giftings are most needed to accomplish a goal.

7. Everyone will be fulfilled as each serves in his/her area of strength.
8. Spiritual and numerical growth will occur as more believers are mentored and released in ministry.
9. Burnout of the leader will be prevented.

OUR STYLE

Sharing influence within teams is highly compatible with women's relational leadership style. At our best, we love seeing as many people as possible involved in a project; we delight in their growth; and we generally aren't threatened by others' suggestions and opinions.

When we are secure in our identity in Christ, we are also less inclined to hoard information—because power is not an issue with us. We aren't afraid to ask those under our leadership, "What would you do if you were I?" because we know this will generate fresh ideas and lead to greater success than we could achieve on our own. We understand that sharing power and information creates loyalty as well, because it tells our teammates that we respect them and their ideas.

Sharing influence through building teams and being inclusive takes more time and makes us vulnerable to criticism, but it also increases cohesive support for any decisions ultimately reached. It reduces the chance that we will be surprised and undermined by unexpected opposition later on.

We will set the course for the next generation of leaders. What we may have to struggle to accomplish through inclusive, participatory leadership will be the norm for those following us, making their way much easier. When we share a common direction and a powerful sense of community, we will get to our destination and accomplish our mission more quickly and easily because our thrust will be boosted by each other's energy. The victory in the end will be that of the Body of Christ!

This is teamwork at its best.

DISCUSSION PROBES:

1. Which more often describes your approach to a project—to do most of the work yourself or to find the people who can assume responsibility for different facets of the project?
   - How much of the activity depends upon your oversight and presence?
2. Draw a "picture" of your ministry, showing the shape of the flow of authority.
   - What are your fears in delegating authority?
   - How will you respond if someone "drops the ball?"
   - Are you empowering others to lead freely?
3. What part does receiving praise play in your decision to delegate?
   - If someone else were praised for implementing a plan that was yours, and he/she gave you no credit, how would you feel?
   - Would you be less inclined to delegate to that person next time?
   - Would you feel "safe" in your leadership position if someone you delegated performed more successfully than you in a particular area?
   - What does it take to desire to see someone else go further than you were able to?
4. List 3 ways by which you keep the vision sharp and clear and help your teammates "own" it.
5. How do you personally build trust within your leadership team?
   - Have you ever taken the time to invite each one to "tell his/her story" to the rest of the team?
   - To what degree can this activity build trust?
6. When you empower and release others, what system of accountability do you use?
7. Share with someone your approach to orchestrating an event such as a women's retreat.
   - Ask them to give you feedback on the strengths of your plan, and to help you discover any possible weaknesses.

8. After reading this chapter, how will you specifically do leadership differently from now on?

9. If "Information equals power," how easy is it for you to share information with others who may use it to then enhance their own position?
   - Do you find yourself hoarding the "inside track" on information?

10. What fear is in your heart when you contemplate team leadership?
    - What is at the root of this fear?

Chapter Six

LEARNING FROM ROLE MODELS

Guard the good deposit that was entrusted to you—
guard it with the help of the Holy Spirit who lives in us.
II Timothy 1:14

Every leader needs help from others more experienced. We must not think that we can forge ahead without heeding the wisdom, example and advice of those who have gone before us in leadership; they have so much to teach us. Furthermore, my experience has been that if I honor godly men and women who have blazed the trail ahead of me, they will lay down their lives to help me mature…and spiritual maturity brings with it leadership responsibility.

Over the twenty-plus years I have been involved directly in ministry, I have served under several leaders, all of whom have taught me *something* profound about influencing others. Some of them demonstrated what harms, but most of them exemplified in some way what heals and brings health to everyone.

Most of my role models in ministry have been men. In fact, it has been very difficult to find female mentors. Those leaders—both men and women from whom I have learned much of value—are Dr. Ken Isom, Sonny Oliver, Dr. Joseph Umidi and Dr. Mara Crabtree.

SELFLESS SERVANT

Ken was the dean who hired me at Teen Challenge, back in the days when he wore one hundred hats and had to be all things to all people. He was not only the Academic Dean, but also the Vocational Director, veterinarian for the 200-acre working farm, preacher, counselor and student disciplinarian. With all the authority he carried, what I remember most about Ken was his humility. He never used power to lead—he simply served compassionately and intelligently—and everyone gladly followed him. God's authority rested upon him; never did he have to demand it for himself.

Ken had left a lucrative veterinary practice to serve at Teen Challenge out of sheer love and compassion for men who had had— or had inflicted upon others—nothing but heartache in life. Although he was a medical doctor and an ordained minister, he arrived at Teen Challenge not demanding the position and power due his educational background, but offering to serve in any way needed.

He was no wimp. But one of my clearest images of Ken was his standing in the dorm hallway with his arm around one of the guy's shoulders, weeping with him and then praying him through to praise. Even though it happened to be an extremely busy day for Ken, he was totally present with this young man, attuned to his plight, never furtively glancing past him hoping for an excuse to escape the fellow's need so he could get on with his next appointment. I noticed that, and I'll never forget it.

Ken always had time for me, too. As green and naïve as I was, he never talked down to me or showed the slightest doubt that I'd be a success. He honored me privately as well as before the men. I didn't do anything to deserve that degree of respect. However, I strove to rise to the level of his expectations and trust because of it.

Years later, when I was preparing to write *Lambs on the Ledge* by sending out questionnaires to leaders I had known, he was one of the few who made the time in his busy schedule to answer. Not only did he respond to my questions, he sent copies of relevant articles and a taped message as well. Every other leader, I had to pursue for a response.

I'm sure Ken had his flaws and shortcomings, but what he taught me of valuing and honoring others, and of being truthful, sincere, soft spoken and selfless, I'll never forget. He was my first mentor in ministry—and one of my best.

FAITHFUL SERVANT

Unlike Ken, who had a strong educational and spiritual heritage, Sonny Oliver had come up through the ranks of the student body at Teen Challenge. He had been a drug addict—illiterate and without purpose for his life. At Teen Challenge, his hunger for God was met, and a vision to minister to others trapped in alcohol and drug addiction was born. He learned to read while in the program and interned after graduation in preparation for a staff position, proving himself faithful every step of the way. Before I left in 1991, Sonny was the Center Director, second in command only to the Executive Director.

He, like Ken, was there to serve, not be served. He loved the students and disciplined with wisdom and discernment. Because he understood the mind and heart of an addict, no one could fool him; but he never made a fool out of any student, no matter how absurd the student's behavior. He was strong in spirit, but gentle, transparent and genuine. He also had a healthy sense of humor, never taking himself too seriously. His love for God and his gratefulness for redemption compelled him to serve with great faithfulness.

I remember something significant Sonny said to me once when having to make a judgment call about a rebellious student's future: "If I must err, I'd rather err on the side of mercy." I also remember, and will be forever grateful for his example, when nearly all the staff turned against a director because of the director's shady business practices and arrogance. Sonny never judged. He simply continued to serve.

When I asked him how he could possibly continue to support a leader in whom everyone else had lost faith, he simply told me, "It's

God's job to judge. I'm here in obedience to God. If God tells me to leave, or if the director asks me to sin, I'll leave. Until then I will honor my authority and serve as unto the Lord." He reminded me of young David who held his own against the negative counsel of his men and simply continued to honor King Saul.

Sonny gave me wise advice on many occasions during the last few years I was there, especially in the areas of knowing who I was in Christ and in defeating arrogance in my own life. I relate those stories in my book, ***Instruments for His Glory.***

PROMOTER OF OTHERS

Years later, when my husband and I moved to Virginia Beach because of his new position as Business Administrator at Kempsville Presbyterian Church, I met Dr. Joseph Umidi. Or rather, he met me. At the time, he was the Executive Pastor at the church as well as Professor of Divinity at nearby Regent University.

Shortly after our arrival, Joseph invited my husband and me out to lunch. It wasn't long into our time together that he began asking me questions about my passion and vision, my experience and the book I had just written, ***Lambs on the Ledge.*** As I shared, he began writing down names of leaders in the area with whom he wanted me to connect.

One of them was John Mannion, founder and then-president of Bible Teachers Institute, now called Tidewater Bible College. After meeting with John, I was asked to write courses for the school based on the issues in ***Lambs on the Ledge***, and then teach them to the many men and women who were studying for the ministry at the school. This opened the door to three years of teaching there, plus ministering with Dr. Umidi and Kevin Hinman, president of Leadership Training International (an affiliate of the Bible college) to church leaders in Murmansk, Russia.

Besides connecting me with these men, Dr. Umidi invited me to speak to the Singles' Ministry at the church and also to his divinity classes at Regent University. His introduction of me to Regent via speaking in his classes has led to some of the most meaningful ministry experiences of my life to date.

COMMUNER WITH GOD

About a year later, Dr. Umidi introduced me to Dr. Mara Crabtree, a gracious pioneer among the faculty in preparing women at Regent for ministry, and the first woman in leadership to speak into my life. Through her invitation, I have become a regular lecturer in the Women's Ministry courses in the School of Divinity.

Mara's very self-controlled and quiet presence reminds me to pursue contemplative worship and communion with God. She models compassion, a listening heart, and a gift for asking the right questions to bring a counselee to self discovery. She never boasts of her own hard-won accomplishments, but asks first about the other's journey.

She is a brilliant woman who first demonstrates love, using knowledge only to enhance another's understanding and to bring clarity. She, like Ken, is a master at giving others her undivided, thoughtful attention—not to impress, but to facilitate meaningful ministry.

THEIR INFLUENCE

These leaders' lives changed my perspective on how leadership should be done. From Ken, I learned that people are more important than agendas, and that compassion must permeate all that we do in ministry. I have found that if I listen well as Ken did, the Holy Spirit brings answers quickly, and often directly to *them*, as I simply give them my undivided attention.

I learned that listening is not a time waster for busy leaders; rather, it is the only way to bear the likeness of Jesus and to remain in touch with the true needs of the world. It teaches us to step out of ourselves and lay our lives down for others.

From Sonny, I learned humble obedience to authority. It is not my job to judge those over me, but to obey, honor and speak well of them, even to God. If they are sinning, I can follow the Matthew 18 principle. When I do, I must be willing to forgive and go with a quiet spirit, only intent upon appealing for change for their sakes and the preservation of their relationship with God.

Sonny had a heart like David toward authority. He modeled

patience and truthfulness, tenderness and loyalty. I needed to see this. These are character qualities I have asked God to develop in my own life and ministry.

Dr. Umidi's influence in my life as a promoter of others has been great. As the Coordinator of Women's Ministries at our church, my focus is not to build my ministry or create a platform for myself, but to seek out others who have a passion to meet a real need within the Body of Christ.

Nothing gives me more pleasure than promoting others and their dreams. I help them craft a plan for implementation, connect them with others of like-passion, champion them publicly and then release them with my blessing. As their coach, I monitor their progress, give counsel when needed, cheer them on and validate them repeatedly in private and in public. I make sure they have whatever they need to do the job well, and continually bring others to them who can broaden their base of effectiveness. In turn, they move out to form their own teams, always looking to raise up, equip and empower others. The team concept permeates everything I espouse and is reinforced today by the example of my pastors at New Life. This I learned first from Dr. Umidi.

I saw that good leaders spread their influence outward, enabling and promoting others. They do not draw influence into themselves and away from others. The more diffused authority is, the more the ministry is owned wholeheartedly by each involved. I am convinced that body ministry must be paramount if we are to be scripturally based and blessed by God for lasting effectiveness. Leader-centered ministry evokes results that do not last—that dissolve when the leader leaves. This is not the way Christ led.

My quest for solitude with God has risen directly from time spent with Mara. In the rush of ministry, we too often miss entirely the mystical beauty and power of being alone with Him simply for the joy of His presence.

I also learned from Dr. Crabtree that solitude is but the engine that drives us, propelling us out to a waiting world. What I hear from God in isolation with Him always contains His whisper to return in confidence to a world that He loves. He fills me with His love, then sends me quickly out to share that love with others. They need to know that He is calling them away to Himself as well.

Mara modeled to me that ministry is not *what* we do, but *who* we are—and that is shaped alone and in unhurried times of solitude with God.

COMMON TRAITS

As I reflect upon these leaders' lives, I see many traits that continue to make their ministries effective and that can give us a pattern to follow as well. These include being:

I. Loyal to Authority
  A. Able to keep their confidences
  B. Positive when speaking about them to others
  C. In prayer for their success
  D. Determined to appeal with a right heart when something is wrong, and then leave judgment to God
  E. Willing to answer truthfully even when the truth might jeopardize their own positions
II. Content
  A. Not power or position hungry
  B. Grateful for their lives and positions
  C. Free from the love of money
  D. Peacemakers
III. Diligent
  A. Able to gather information and make decisions
  B. Prompt and organized
  C. On the lookout for ways to improve
IV. Concerned for Others
  A. Gentle and forbearing
  B. Quick to forgive
  C. Willing to go the extra mile to understand and help
  D. Effective listeners
  E. Willing to defend someone falsely accused
V. Cheerfully Obedient
  A. Not critical
  B. Committed to fulfill a larger goal than their own agendas

C. Quick to grasp the vision behind an order
VI. Able to Take Correction
    A. Not defensive nor given to anger
    B. Able to say they are wrong and are willing to change
    C. Aware that constructive criticism of their work is not an attack on them personally
VII. Promoters of others; unconcerned with self-promotion
    A. Selfless
    B. Delighted to network for others' sake
    C. Excited at others' successes
VIII. Meek
    A. Able to discern when to speak and when not to, based upon what is best for the other person
    B. Yielded to the Holy Spirit in temperament
    C. Able to weigh differing opinions
IX. Free from Bitterness
    A. Cleansed of old injuries through forgiveness
    B. Strong in their devotional lives; growing daily in Christ
    C. Convinced that they have been forgiven much, therefore free to love much
X. In Possession of Personal Integrity
    A. Faithful to their families; honoring them always, cheering them on
    B. Respectful of others—helping them hear God for themselves, not giving them all the answers
    C. Concerned about their neighbors and community
    D. Truthful and honest in personal affairs

IN THE DAYS AHEAD

As a result of being blessed by the examples of such men and women, I strive to model what I have seen in them to those coming after me in leadership. I long to influence others in the same godly ways they influenced me.

I constantly watch for *more* such men and women from whose walk to glean, and I will forever thank God for those sentinels of wisdom He posts along my way. Whenever possible, I request time with the leaders of successful ministries in my geographic area. I approach them armed with thoughtful questions about what they feel is most important—and most difficult—in ministry leadership, what God has been teaching them most recently, their vision for the future, and what or who has been of the greatest influence during the past five years.

By God's grace, I will imitate godly men and women as they imitate Christ, until His life reigns unhindered in mine.

(See *OUR BIBLICAL MENTORS IN LEADERSHIP*
in the Appendix.)

DISCUSSION PROBES:

1. Select someone who has greatly influenced your life for good.
   - List the strengths of this person and describe how he/she has shaped your thinking and ministry.
   - What was his/her attitude toward those just emerging on the ministry and/or leadership scene?
   - If they are still living, write them a letter of appreciation.
2. Do you actively promote others, connecting them with people who have the influence to further their cause?
   - Describe a situation where you promoted another, was promoted by someone else or observed it being done effectively.
3. How well do you listen to others?
   - Develop a mental plan to use to quiet yourself when someone wants to speak with you and you are in a hurry.
   - How can you determine when the issue needs to be assigned to an appointment rather than an impromptu conversation?
4. What is the difference between solitude with God and your "quiet time" in the Word and prayer?
   - What are you doing to work solitude into your schedule?
   - How would listening for God in solitude improve your listening skills with other people?
5. Describe your progress at learning how to ask questions that help those who come to you for counsel to explore and discover their own answers from the Lord.
   - Are you trying to cease being an "Answer lady" for everyone?
6. Why is gathering influence to yourself more stressful—if not impossible—than enabling others' promotion?
7. Describe Jesus' example of sharing His influence with His disciples.
   - To whom did Jesus want everyone to look for direction?
8. Explain this statement: "Ministry is not *what* we do, but *who* we are."
9. Describe situations in which you are mentoring others as you have been mentored.

- Are you being anyone's champion?
- How are you doing this?

10. Take time to discuss the list of qualities listed in the chapter.
    - Where are you strong?
    - Where are you weak?

Pray with someone about the weak areas and develop a plan to improve.

Chapter Seven

DEVELOPING OTHERS

And the things you have heard me say in the presence of many witnesses entrust to reliable men who will also be qualified to teach others. II Timothy 2:2

At its heart, ministry leadership *is not* about wielding authority or power, but about energizing others for a godly purpose with a redemptive end. Leadership today is not defined by those who move mountains single-handedly—building ministries that disappear when they do—but by those who set the pattern of investing in others, drawing them into the work and preparing them to go even farther than the leaders themselves have been able to go. In this way, ministry effectiveness endures and grows, anchored in obedience to God and integrity rather than in a personality.

JESUS' EXAMPLE

Jesus developed men and women for ministry on several levels. On the most personal level, He mentored the three who were most intimate with Him—Peter, James and John—to know His very heart. On the next level, He coached the twelve together to be dynamic world changers. Then he taught, by His lifestyle of love, His friends and all those who followed Him from town to town.

Jesus not only knew what He wanted them to become, but He knew and valued their needs. He communicated deeply and patiently with them, never belittling them for what they sincerely did not know. And He expected growth as He, precept upon precept, taught them by example and illustration.

In the end, they not only loved Him to the death, but they came to understand and emulate Him to such a fine degree that the whole world today has been able to grasp His purpose and plan. Those who had known Him first-hand truly turned the world upside down!

PERSONAL DEVELOPMENT FIRST

Of greatest significance was what Jesus was on the inside. And so it is with us today. Our integrity and character—or lack of it— will influence those we mentor and coach more greatly than all the words of instruction we can give. But character and integrity do not just magically appear in our lives. They come from passing the tests of life—by applying godly principles when our feet are held to the fire in times of crisis. Character and integrity grow as we obey Him and count the cost to be His disciples.

Before we invest in others, we need to build a lifestyle of investing in our *own* personal and spiritual growth. We are models to all who will follow in our wake. As we realized in Chapter One, passion is not enough to prove we are capable, worthy leaders. We must have hearts that pursue God diligently and lives that are being conformed to His image.

In fact, whether we want to see spiritual changes occur in those who follow us, or in our organization, we must first invite God to change us. As people around us begin to see the results of our own personal growth in the desired direction, we will gain both credibility and respect. With those two things, change in the others we influence will not just be possible, but probable.

Every leader needs a Personal Growth Plan to help produce the fruit of a disciplined and spiritually mature life, and to grow professionally. Sharing out of such a life as *this* provokes greatness in the lives of those who are learning from us.

There are at least four areas in which we need to be continually learning and growing. They include:

1.Spiritual—by pursuing intimacy with God through worship, Bible study, reflection, prayer, solitude and fasting.

2.Professional—by being mentored, taking courses, attending seminars, reading relevant books and listening to tapes and dialoging with other professionals.

3.Relational—by time spent with friends and family, sharing affection, listening and caring.

4.Physical—by exercising and eating properly.

Each of us needs to establish goals for these areas that are pursued daily or weekly. As my Sr. Pastor, Dave Earley, stresses, such goals need to be SMART: Specific and simple, measurable, attainable, relevant and time-oriented.

Below is a sample daily chart:

Week of _____

Spiritual	Professional	Relational	Physical
1 hr. in the Word, prayer & reflection	Rd. 1 ch. of a book on leadership	Meet a friend for lunch	1/2 hr. power walk

OUR NEED FOR MENTORING

Sandy joyfully accepted the position of Missions Director at Pine Bluff Community Church, but after two weeks on the job at this fast-paced, growing church, she knew that she needed help. While she had a degree in missions, had been on several short-term mission trips as a teen and had the administrative skills needed for the job, she sensed a lack of long-range vision and clear understanding of how to multiply the effectiveness of her department. She had been pursuing a Personal Growth Plan that had included books on leadership development, but she needed someone's personal touch who could identify with her situation.

Because leadership development was not yet an intentional goal of her church, she had to look elsewhere for mentoring. Wisely, she began calling missions directors in churches the size of Pine Bluff and larger, praying for God to connect her with someone who could mentor her in vision casting and creating a culture in her department of raising up and training leaders that would increase future productivity. These were her greatest needs. She was convinced that God had called her to this position at this time, but she needed exposure to someone more experienced.

At a local missions conference, she met Joe and Donna Caffet from a church not far away that was well known for its highly-developed missions program. After sharing her frustration with them over dinner the last night of the conference, they retired to the lounge to pray for God's direction in their relationship. By the time they finished praying, the Caffets were convinced that God wanted them to begin mentoring Sandy. The next week, they met for the first time to begin the process of setting growth goals and sharing their wisdom and experience with her. As the weeks wore on, Sandy grew dramatically as a leader.

BOTTOM LINE

As we seek mentors, we must first and foremost look for mature individuals whose strength as leaders emanate from lives of integrity. Such individuals will be willing to strike deeply against any character flaw or egocentric tendencies in our own lives. They will deal with real issues. They will work with us to formulate a plan for meaningful change and growth and uncover areas in need of improvement.

All of us need the input, challenge and accountability that come from being mentored by someone more experienced, even if it's sporadic or short-termed. By the same token, God expects us to be mentoring and coaching those under *our* influence. Because leadership is not about promoting ourselves, we are called to be continually looking for ways to facilitate the growth and development of the future leaders around us. As *we* develop, our expertise can be multiplied out and into those around us so that all may be equipped to minister to the incredible volume of needs in the Body of Christ, and be ready to accommodate the great harvest God is preparing.

MY EXPERIENCE

Mentoring is designed to be for specific reasons and for a predetermined length of time. Growth occurs most readily in someone who hungers for it and doggedly pursues the expertise of someone who is already highly successful in his/her field.

At New Life, mentoring is an important part of the intentional process of growing leaders. Because future leaders are chosen for their commitment to the vision, heart for God, emerging gifts and desire to learn, mentoring comes naturally. It is the indispensable link between each level of leadership.

When I took the position at New Life, I did so with the understanding that I would be able to meet with, and be mentored by, the Sr. Pastor. I wanted first-hand explanations of where the church was going so that, as the Women's Ministries grew, I could be sure we were in direct line with the Sr. Pastor's vision. Even more than that, I wanted to glean from his many years of experience in this church environment. I usually went prepared with an agenda of questions for him, my goals and an update on any event that was in the planning stage. He listened, offered insights and occasionally warned against a specific action or attitude. He shared his experiences to deepen my understanding of the ramifications of each action. In response, I adjusted my attitude or plan, asked more questions and took notes.

When we met, our focus was primarily on the overall motive and momentum of the ministry, application of principles in all activities and relationships, and my own personal growth.

Sometimes he had a fresh objective to review with me, but more often, he asked questions about how I was doing spiritually and about the progress being made with the next level of leaders that I was mentoring, as well as the small group leaders that I was coaching. We discussed vision and strategy and, of course, my Personal Growth Plan. As a member of the church leadership team, I had to submit my Six-Months' Ministry Goals each January and June for his review. He then could hold me accountable for them. I was in a very real sense being walked through my own development as a future leader of leaders.

After I had gained strength and confidence in the position, we decided to meet less frequently and more for feedback and evaluation. However, since all the pastors and directors participate in leadership training as a group with him twice every month, the mentoring has actually broadened to include melding us together as a team, even as we grow in expertise individually. In this context, we are stretched and challenged on a continuing basis, while having a forum for sharing ideas and frustrations. Here we also have opportunity to pray for one another on a very personal level. It is a tremendous blessing for each of us.

COACHING

On the other hand, coaching brings more direct oversight of functions. Coaches ask more than they tell, challenging us to explore and discover more effective ways of doing the work of ministry. The Small Groups Pastor at New Life, Rod Dempsey, currently coaches me on the *details* of training and equipping small group leaders—those in the trenches ministering to the women God brings into their groups. He meets with me to brainstorm, plan and guide me as we discuss creative approaches. He also challenges me to integrate my goals with other department heads to prevent fragmentation. He cheers me on, helps me stay the course, provokes my thinking and helps me stretch to meet the goals of this organization for growth and discipleship.

DEVELOPING OTHERS

Peter Drucker has made the statement that "No executive has ever suffered because his people were strong and effective." As leaders, our call is first to find others with like passion, a variety of giftings, a hunger to learn and grow and a track record of sensitivity to God. As these people are developed into the best leaders they can be, they will produce other great leaders. We must set into motion an unstoppable succession of sharing influence, calling forth the highest and best in others and empowering them to step out with expertise.

We will multiply our effectiveness as we draw them into our hearts and share the mission because they bring wonderful skills and insights to the mix. The end result will be more powerful than the sum of the "parts" we each play. It establishes a marvelous and energizing spirit of interdependency.

By setting a new climate of passion and purpose, we will attract others who thrive in that climate. As we stay focused on God's plan for our particular ministry, God will bring others to us who share our vision and core values. Their hearts will leap when they learn of the mission we are on, and they will long to join us. They will be our greatest assets. If we develop them as leaders, as we have been developed, they will dream with us for the seemingly impossible to come true and will serve in spite of hardship and opposition.

PRACTICAL APPLICATION

Our influence can radiate out on several levels. At New Life, a church based on small groups, I wear several hats. I cast vision, spearhead special events such as conferences, retreats, seminars, outings and praise celebrations as well as raise up leaders for all our ministries.

Of greatest impact spiritually and relationally upon our women are our Women's Life Groups (open and multipliable), Classes (of 8-10 weeks duration, each focusing on a specific core issue for women), and Freedom Groups (of 8-10 weeks duration, for recovery or support). Each of the groups has a leader or teacher and at least one apprentice who desires to someday be the leader of her own group or class. At the same time, I am mentoring four women, each of whom has successfully led a group or taught a class and who now coaches three groups. I continue to coach the remaining groups and classes for whom I do not yet have coaches. But my goal is to be able to turn over coaching of all 16 small groups to five coaches by next spring, which will release me to concentrate on pouring my life into these coaches. In five years, as the church doubles, I expect to have ten in place. As the women throughout the ministry move from one level to the next, they will raise up others to take their places. As I sow into them, they sow into others coming along.

WHY BOTHER?

Mentoring and coaching take great energy and commitment. They require a tremendous amount of time and planning. But the results are astounding and worth it all! And never can we escape the echo of Jesus' words to His disciples: *"The harvest is plentiful, but the workers are few. Ask the Lord of the harvest, therefore, to send out workers into his harvest field."* Matt. 9:37.

Effectively mobilizing laborers to sow, water and reap is a powerful and rewarding experience. No longer is the work limited to what we alone can offer, but we have multiplied our gifts and passion out and equipped others in such a way that virtual mountains can be removed in the name of God.

Indeed, the fields are white; we must waste no time in becoming efficient. As we recognize the gravity of the task and determine to develop those around us, we must first pray: "Lord, guide me to those You know are ready to press on in You. Grant me favor as I pour my life and expertise into them. Keep me learning each step of the way. Make us all into *Your* likeness, governed by *Your* sweet and powerful Spirit. Continually remind me that my own promotion is not what will get the enormous job facing us done—but rather an army of your people sharing influence and information, strengthening one another in love and wisdom."

It is sometimes hard to tell where mentoring ends and coaching begins because either can help others walk through every difficult situation and come out with greater strength and wisdom.

But, in general:

1. Mentoring will invest in someone for his or her personal growth, while coaching prepares someone for a specific task.
2. Mentoring is transformational and is a gift without strings attached, while coaching is an exchange of challenging ideas and produces skill growth.
3. Mentoring is governed by the *person's* needs, while coaching is based largely on the *organization's* needs.
4. Mentoring deepens our understanding of ourselves and the call of God on our lives, while coaching helps create plans of action and assesses progress in achieving them.

Whether we are receiving or giving mentoring and coaching, we must know exactly where the goal line is before we start. Areas that need improvement must be uncovered, plans for meaningful change and growth are necessary and implementation of strategy is critical. We may at times have to be willing to risk relationships in order to deal with real issues. But if love and trust have been part of the equation from the start, deep growth will occur and our goals can be reached.

IN CONCLUSION

A culture of mentoring and coaching nurtures leadership. As personal growth, team spirit and passion for the cause converge, leaders come forth. When God brings women of influence to our attention, let's try to get to know them quickly. Let's seek out the passion that burns in their hearts, help them form personal growth plans and stir up their spiritual gifts. Then we must do all we can to cultivate the potential in them that matches the potential of the ministry, while *never forgetting to care more for them as individuals than for the gifts they bring.*

As we help others reach their highest potential, we can look forward to the day when they will be ready to take our places in leadership of the ministries of tomorrow!

DISCUSSION PROBES:

1. Define in your own words the purpose of ministry leadership.
2. How are you investing in your own spiritual and professional development right now?
3. Create a Personal Growth Plan for yourself. Remember to make it simple, measurable, appropriate, realistic and time-oriented.
4. Who has been a mentor to you? Describe their value to you.
5. If you plan to ask someone to mentor you, list the needs you have that match that person's strengths. This will guide you in defining the role you would like him/her to play in your growth.
6. What attitude and behaviors are necessary if you as a leader and those you lead are to be interdependent?
7. What can be divisive or threatening to either of you when you attempt interdependency?
8. Describe the differences, in you own words, between mentoring and coaching.
9. How can coaching be applied effectively to your own sphere of influence right now?
10. Describe the goal line for this season in your life and ministry.

Chapter Eight

ACCOUNTABILITY
AND INTERCESSION

Whoever gives heed to instruction prospers,
and blessed is he who trusts in the Lord.
Proverbs 16:20.

Pray also for me, that whenever I open my mouth,
words may be given me so that I will fearlessly
make known the mystery of the gospel...
Ephesians 6:19

There is probably no more dangerous place to be without a guide or a rear guard than on the battlefield of ministry leadership. The bodies of fallen or disenchanted leaders who have tried to go it alone litter the rocky terrain. No one is safe from the enemy's attacks; no one has eyes in the back of his or her head; and no one has perfect insight into every situation. We need each other, and we need help.

ACCOUNTABILITY PARTNERS

Especially in para-church ministries (organizations that are not churches, but complement the work of churches by specializing in an area of outreach), leaders often "fly by the seat of their pants!" There is too often no central plan of accountability; the focus is on *outcome* rather than on the process of personal growth. It is difficult to have a productive or enduring discipleship plan in effect in an "end justifies the means" ministry atmosphere. Mismanagement and ethical failures within such ministries are great and frequent.

Within the last few years, leaders have finally become very receptive to being held personally accountable for their ministry practices, home life and spiritual growth. Across the country, men and women in positions of authority have sought and found mature individuals who are now alongside them, helping them stay pure and on target in all areas of their lives, even within the fluctuating makeup of the average para-church ministry.

Of course, the success of this endeavor hinges both upon each leader's willingness to be open and honest with his or her accountability person, and that person's willingness to maintain confidentiality and love for the leader. Although secrets and hidden agendas have a way of coming to light in often dramatic, humiliating ways, transparency is required if they are to be aired and stripped of their power before they hurt someone, and confidentiality is necessary for the leader to continue to trust and remain vulnerable.

To be held accountable requires getting together on a regular basis—usually once or twice a month—with phone calls, if needed, in between. (If the partner lives nearby, the meetings can be more frequent.) The accountability partner signs on with us for the long haul, seriously agreeing to listen well, ask probing questions and help us set goals, monitor our interior progress and scrutinize our passion. This may be the same person who prayed with us through the events of our past (See Chapter One), but can be any mature believer of the same sex, who is willing to know us deeply and can understand what we have been dealing with in our lives. It is amazing how freeing it is to have honest, sincere encouragement—as well as rebuke—when necessary.

As we model a lifestyle of accountability to our teammates and explain the benefits, they too will catch the vision and seek such relationships. This will encourage new believers within our organizations to join discipleship groups, such as small Bible studies in which they can be known well, or link up with a mature woman who will help them apply the Word to their own personal growth in the faith. Later, when they become qualified to lead, they will naturally value accountability.

If I were a leader of a para-church ministry, I would not employ anyone who was not actively serving and known well within a local church body. Too much can be hidden in a para-church ministry; accountability works best in the local church.

TEAM ACCOUNTABILITY

In a larger, corporate sense, as leaders we need to have in place an effective pattern of working through projects that automatically builds in the kind of accountability that prevents personal, as well as team, failure. *Accountability at its best helps us all succeed,* rather than focuses on our potential weaknesses.

Before any project is begun:

1. Clearly explain the purpose.
2. Dialog to determine strategy.
3. Assign responsibility according to gifting and interest.
4. Make expectations of outcome clear.
5. Establish timetable for reporting progress.

Then:

6. Reconvene at intervals to encourage and work out any problems that might have surfaced.
7. Pray for one another daily.
8. Praise authentically.
9. Provide assistance for anyone who is faltering.
10. Celebrate together the team's success, and reward integrity.
11. Debrief a few days later to assess strengths and weaknesses

of the project and make note of ways to improve.

The focus of every project must ultimately be to turn the hearts of people toward God, or the project will take on a life of its own. Participants will more likely become territorial and above correction if their motive is anything but to glorify God and make Him known. If we can keep everyone's vision out ahead on that desired result, all will pull together, compromise on their differences and applaud each other's success much more readily.

INTERCESSORS

Besides personal and team accountability, we need powerful and consistent prayer. A circle of intercessors who will pray with us about ministry issues and personal decisions is essential. They will fight for us in prayer during hard times or when we are under attack by the enemy because of the ground God is gaining through our faithfulness to the call. These intercessors need to share our vision and be kept constantly abreast of our activities, challenges and victories. To be most effective in prayer for us, they must be men and women who know how to pray in the Spirit and discern His direction, and have their own lives in order. Their commitment to pray for us is a serious one; it will require discipline and faithfulness.

THE JERICHO PRAYER CIRCLE

I personally have been blessed with seven godly women who have committed themselves to pray for me daily. I keep them constantly apprised of all that is happening in my life and ministry so they can pray with precision. From time to time, they also speak prophetically into my life, encouraging and exhorting me. I could not be in ministry without such prayer partners.

A few years ago, the Lord gave one of my intercessors, D. Kirkland, a beautiful design for shaping an effective prayer circle for any given leader. She named it the *Jericho Prayer Circle*, and it is the plan we use. Each partner, plus the leader, filled out a Profile Sheet on herself which outlined her daily prayer needs. D. then entered these requests on a grid that set the week up in such a way that each woman prays each day for a different partner and her specific needs for that day, as well as the leader's (my) specific needs *every* day. In this way, everyone is getting prayed for each day by one other partner plus the leader, and is praying for one *other* partner plus the leader. I, as the leader, pray alternately for the partners, a different one each day; however, I am prayed for by everyone, every day. As the leader, I may also send them, via email, special requests that come up from time to time, that go beyond my set daily request.

While the primary purpose of the *Jericho Prayer Circle* is to lift up and protect the leader, all the women are intertwined with one another in prayer in a systematic way. Everyone benefits by blessing and being blessed.

The plan God gave D. eliminates wondering how, what and for whom to pray. It is a tremendous time-saving strategy which allows for more time directly in prayer.

CONVENIENCE

D. also designed a 3"x3" tri-fold "brochure" that lists who is praying for us on which days, whom *we* are to pray for on those days, what we are to pray specifically for, and a statement of the purpose of the plan on the back. We each have three copies of the booklet that fit nicely inside our Bibles, can be taped to our mirrors or kept on our desks or in our purses. I always have one within reach wherever I am. In a matter of seconds, I can see for whom I am to be praying and for what, and pray on the spot!

KNIT TOGETHER

One of the most beautiful benefits of the *Jericho Prayer Circle* is that all eight of us have become closely knit together through praying for each other. We are all involved in ministries in different churches and often don't get to see each other more than four or five times a year, yet we love each other deeply. When I moved away from Virginia Beach a few years ago, I feared they would all desert me! But we are closer than ever, even though I live in Ohio, and they are still in Virginia. Distance is not a problem.

STAYING CLOSE

Every year, we all travel back to Virginia Beach for our own prayer retreat together. Whether it's at a retreat center or in a home, it's wonderful! We worship together, laugh and cry together, pray for one another and hear confirmation and words of wisdom for one another from the Lord. The ministry that takes place by and to one another is astounding in its completeness. The Holy Spirit touches all of us in meaningful and refreshing ways.

And after we part and I am far away from them physically, I feel as though I am literally being carried on the wings of their prayers. How I cherish these godly women and their faithfulness! How I love being faithful to them!

GREAT FOR PASTORS' WIVES

The pastors' wives at my former church in North Carolina also adopted the plan for themselves, encircling the senior pastor's wife. They had been meeting for prayer for one another previously, but without any organization of the requests—and since they were very busy themselves—prayer had been haphazardly carried out once they went home. Using this plan, they were not overwhelmed with all the requests everyday, but could concentrate on just one per day and cover everyone in prayer by the end of the week.

ADAPTABLE FOR WOMEN'S MINISTRIES

Recently, I introduced the *Jericho Prayer Circle* to the Women's Ministry in my own church here in Ohio. Instead of having seven ladies surround one leader, we simply set up circles of eight without a leader, each praying around the circle for one another. My leadership team and I are in one to support one another in a very focused way.

It is a great plan to interlock all the women in any ministry and bring unity, as well as to foster continuity and the release of the power of God into everyone's life.

Whether used by a leadership team, pastors' wives or the pastors themselves, friends, or entire ministries, it is a very practical way to supernaturally care for one another.

The bottom line is: We *need* one another for protection, encouragement, correction and to keep us grounded in God's love and in reality. These are all found within trusted accountability and faithful intercession. To neglect these is to invite, at the worst, destruction by the enemy and, at the best, great loneliness, neither of which we want.

(All the material needed to set up *Jericho Prayer Circles* within your organization can be secured directly from D. Kirkland via email at dkbyfaith@yahoo.com)

DISCUSSION PROBES:

1. Have you ever been in an accountability relationship?
   - If so, describe the positives and negatives of the experience.
   - How could it have been done more effectively?
2. How close must your accountability partner be to your current ministry position to be effective?
3. Is there anything you don't want an accountability partner to know about you?
   - How can secrets impede the success of accountability?
4. What, if any, are the limitations of a man holding you accountable?
   - What dangers are inherent in a male-female personal accountability relationship?
   - Are there areas for which a man *can* hold you accountable?
5. What are the necessary boundaries within any accountability partnership, whether with a man or a woman, to protect both of you from unhealthy emotional bonding or dependence?
6. Who prays for you daily?
   - Do you take the time to keep them regularly apprised of your activities so that they can pray for you effectively?
7. Seriously consider the *Jericho Circle* format discussed in this chapter.
   - What would be the benefits of the *Jericho Circle* for your ministry?
   - How soon could you implement it, if that is your plan?
8. Plan a spiritual retreat with those who pray for you.
9. If you don't already do so, begin to pray regularly for someone else's ministry so that you retain a corporate view of ministry and avoid myopic vision.
10. Journal your prayer requests and answers to prayer.
    - Hold Celebrations of Praise and Prayer on a regular basis.

Chapter Nine

BALANCE
AND FOCUS

*I will instruct you and teach you
in the way you should go;
I will counsel you and watch over you.*
Psalm 32:8

Women are notorious for being able to do a million things at once, but as leaders, we must focus on those activities that we do best. By building strong teams that possess a wide range of gifts, we can safely delegate the functions for which we are least needed. Then we can concentrate on our strengths and perform with excellence.

Everywhere I go, I sense God saying to us that we must develop a laser sharp focus for ministry, letting involvement that isn't germane to the vision He has given us fall away. We can no longer afford to spread our energy over a dozen pursuits simply because we love doing them. We must define everything we do by the vision and mission God is mandating for our lives at this time.

I personally feel the effects of this fact when I am orchestrating a conference and long to be on the worship team as well. Before becoming a staff member at New Life, I played keyboard and sang on a worship team in Pennsylvania. I loved ministering to others in that way! But now I am the host and coordinator, helping others find their places of ministry. It's a "death" that is real to me as I keep my eyes on God's present mandate for my life. But it is a joy, truly, to see others experience what I enjoyed years ago.

WHEN WE DO IT ALL

There are at least four dangers connected with running our legs off in ministry:

1. Others who need to develop their gifts won't step forward.
2. We fall into pride and deception, believing we are indispensable and that the ministry would fall apart without our endless service or control.
3. We gradually find ourselves running on old steam, then no steam. At this point, we will begin to resent those around us who are doing little, take offense easily and neglect seeking God for decisions.
4. Many "good" things become the enemy of the "best" and in our exhaustion, we lose focus and our passion withers.

PROTECTING THE HOME FRONT

When we are too involved in the ministry, our friends and families feel slighted and powerless to stop our self-destructive drive. While resentment builds on the ministry front within our own hearts, because our imbalance has made us susceptible to the high demands and expectations of others, resentment also festers on the home front. Family relationships and close friendships are fragile and can wither under the heat of neglect. They must be continually watered and nurtured, and this takes time.

When our children are still at home, they are without doubt, our priority. If ministry causes our time with them to be hurried and frustrating, we are doing too much. If we can't attend any of our kids' ballgames or concerts, there's something wrong. There must be balance. Staying at home with them as much as possible will yield the most wonderful memories of our lives. Long after ministries have come and gone, our families will be there. The quality of our relationships with them in the future will depend upon the intentional consideration we give them now.

Even if it seems as though our kids will never pass out of childhood, this time will indeed be gone all too quickly. They *will* grow up and leave home. Yes, we *will* have scores of our best years left after they are grown! While they are young, our greatest focus must be on *them*—the ones for whom we are most responsible to disciple—in loving patience and creativity. What a treasure they are to God!

STOPPING THE TRAIN

When I was on staff at a discipleship ministry in Bradenton, Florida, several years ago, I did nearly *everything*. I taught the Christian Living classes, booked meetings, counseled, directed the choir, sat on the discipline committee, occasionally led church meetings and even gave haircuts. In grassroots ministry, this is often the case in the beginning. But this pattern should not persist long into the ministry's growth. If it does, it is an indication that we are not focusing properly on raising up more leaders and are allowing the "tyranny of the urgent" to rule.

God's call for me to quit this craziness in order to begin writing birthed a new concept of ministry within me. God knows when we have had enough.

REDEFINING FOCUS

There comes a point in each of our lives and ministries when God challenges us to narrow our focus. Often preceding this narrowing of focus, God will draw us into a period of solitude with Himself. And if we won't withdraw willingly, He'll allow the inevitable crisis to evict us from our "doing." The very ministry in which we have buried ourselves may fall apart! But most commonly, our withdrawal is precipitated simply by a growing hunger in our hearts to be alone with God for extended periods of time. Ministry pales in comparison to the urgency of each of these developments. We are either forced or drawn to pull away from activity to reassess our vision and mission and hear from Him.

As we relinquish our "roles" and relax in His presence, realigning our lives with His priorities, the Holy Spirit will effect subtle changes in our hearts to prepare us for the next stage of ministry.

BE HONEST

Because our culture is constantly challenging us as women to rise in the corporate world, compete with men and prove ourselves intellectually and professionally, we need to keep close tabs on our motives for desiring to lead in ministry. Are they pure? Or are they an outcropping of our insecurities and our lack of knowing our value in God's eyes—with or without doing something "great?"

Is our longing for professional growth masking a deep discontentment with our husbands or current bosses, or a lack of recognition as a person of great worth in life? Do we have unresolved conflicts that drive us to pursue spiritual leadership to prove a point? Are we running from repressed anger that needs to be confessed, or is there forgiveness and repentance that must come forth so that healing can come at last?

DISCONTENTMENT IN MINISTRY

Even when we are in the thick of highly significant ministry and there has been no violation of balance in our lives, discontentment and frustration can crop up and sap our inspiration and energy.

Brenda, a wonderful lady, whose children were grown and who knew well the dynamics of leadership and management, found herself in a leadership role in a large prayer ministry. While prayer was her greatest passion and she was very capable of performing her job, she was becoming increasingly miserable in the position.

She began having nightmares, panic attacks and stomach problems, and became very irritated by the leadership tactics of her superiors. While she loved the job and the ministry, she hated what was happening to her.

She invited me to give a seminar for the ministry. The second day, I taught on the most common reasons for discontentment in the ministry. They are that:

1. We have unresolved conflict. Disappointments have turned to resentment.
2. We are not focused; we spend too much time ministering outside the area of our gifting.
3. We haven't developed the expertise for our position and are in over our heads.
4. We took the job for the wrong reason.
5. The season for serving—either in this ministry or in the current area of specialization—has ended. A new chapter is about to be written in our lives.

At the end of the session, Brenda came down the aisle and with tears in her eyes, took the microphone and informed her co-workers that she was going to resign! Walking away from that job was the last things she had expected to do that day, but as she had listened to the reasons I gave for discontentment, she realized the root of her unrest. She had simply taken the job for the wrong reason: the prestige and money, which had also influenced her husband's counsel to her to take the position. She had furthermore realized that she was not operating in her primary calling, which was to pray.

She definitely had the skills to lead, but it wasn't where her passion lay during this season of her life. She knew she must reassess everything about the direction of her ministry. She had to resign in order to do this.

What relief poured over her! She then withdrew into an extended period of solitude with God, becoming rejuvenated in His presence. A year or so later, she and her husband were asked to help a local pastor begin a new church. She moved easily into the position of intercessor and ministry advisor. All her illnesses had, of course, disappeared. She was completely at peace, in the center of God's will, with an appropriate and laser sharp focus to her calling.

STAYING TOO LONG

Over the years, I have witnessed many cases of men and women remaining in ministry positions too long. A. W. Tozer said once that Christians have a hard time knowing when to begin a work, but an even harder time knowing when to quit.

One problem that stands in the way of our discerning God's timing is that we always want to know the next destination before we are willing to relinquish the security of the familiar, even when we are becoming more and more discontent. We doggedly hang on, making matters worse. If God would just lay out the next step for us, we'd be glad to leave!

But God rarely makes obedience that easy. If our future were all clearly marked out for us, there would be no need to trust Him. And if we drift from complete dependence upon Him, it won't be long before we are completely alone and out of His will, unable to hear His voice anymore.

Another problem is that we too often derive our identity from our ministry positions and are secretly frightened at the thought of releasing that identity. Who would we be without it?

But that is exactly the question God wants us to face. *If it is not enough to be His child and be known only to Him, we have no business being in His service.* If it is *our* presence and power we are promoting, *His* presence and power will abandon us. He must remove us before we defile others with our arrogance and idolatry of ministry.

GUIDELINES TO PREVENT OVEREXTENSION:

1. Never commit to do anything, no matter how appealing, on the spot.
2. Put our families before ministry. If we lose them, we lose our hearts and our credibility.
3. Test an activity against our mission statements. Is it within the

focus God has ordained for this season?

4. Delegate to others everything possible. Do only what we alone can do.
5. Have accountability partners who understand us and the pressures we are under, as well as the nature of the ministry. Take their counsel!
6. Guard both quality time with friends and family—and, of course, with God.
7. Intentionally schedule time for something that is simply entertaining, relaxing or fun each week.
8. Ask ourselves periodically: Is it time for me to release this position to someone else and wait on God for my next assignment?

THE IMPORTANCE OF HOW WE LEAVE

The manner and spirit in which we leave a ministry is often more telling than how we have served.

For over a year, Jennifer had been restless in her leadership position at a large, independent church in the Southeast. In her discontentment, instead of realizing that it was time for her to go, she focused on the pastors, imagining slights and abuses on every hand.

Her vision grew narrow and her service became labor aimed at forcing others to see how important she was. Her critical attitude defiled the ministry, intimidated many and caused everyone to wish her gone. She became a foe of the ministry she had once loved.

She was eventually undone by her attitude, and she had to resign. If she had recognized a year earlier that her season there was up and had resigned then, she could have left well-loved and blessed. She stayed too long and left poorly. All her years of service were eclipsed by her ingratitude during her last months on the job. Whether any of her accusations were justified didn't matter in the end; her lack of integrity in not repenting, forgiving and blessing those with whom she had ministered made her word of no account.

I'm convinced that, for most of us, 10-12 years is the longest God will keep us in one position. In *Jesus CEO*, Laurie Beth Jones writes that, "Leaders constantly look for ways to expand their visions, their influence and their contribution." This usually requires either a change of position, of focus or of ministry.

We must be continually growing in our sensitivity to what God is planning next. As we learn more about His ways and deepen in our personal reliance upon Him and His purposes, our horizons will expand. Fresh ideas, higher goals, greater ministry influence will inspire us to step out of our comfort zones and attempt new challenges for the kingdom. We must be an adventurous sort to be in God's company!

But always, He will require balance in our lives. If we get our priorities confused; if we let conflict go unresolved; if we take our identity from our work; and if we become bitter or great in our own eyes—*no matter how talented we are*—He will allow our worlds to crash around us, for our sake and for the sake of those who love us. How much wiser to carefully watch and guard our hearts, surrender our egos, have our eyes on our servant-savior and do only what *He* wants us to do during each season of our lives!

(Read more about leaving well, including repentance and restoration, in ***Lambs on the Ledge.***)

DISCUSSION PROBES:

1. There are seasons in a woman's life. In which of the following are you now?
   - Dreaming
   - Preparing
   - Waiting
   - Parenting
   - Launching
   - Ministering part-time
   - Ministering full-time
   - Retreat and solitude
2. How is God using your present season to teach you balance?
3. If God is asking you to narrow your focus, what must fall away or be delegated to someone else?
4. Honestly evaluate your present motives for wanting to be in leadership. What second-love motives may have crept in?
5. Like Brenda in this chapter, have you ever taken a position in ministry for the wrong reason? What was that reason?
6. Have you ever witnessed someone over-staying their season in a certain position or ministry?
   - What happened to that person's attitude when he/she became restless?
   - Has it ever happened to you?
   - What have you learned that you can use in the future?
7. Why is it important to "end well?"
8. Study the GUIDELINES TO PREVENT OVEREXTENSION on p. 109-109.
   - Which ones particularly strike a chord with you as a current need or caution?
9. Change always adds new learning experiences.
   - What did you learn from your most recent change in ministry or leadership?
   - What, if anything, do you wish you had done differently in the way you handled the change?
10. How can talent and humility interplay successfully?

Section Three:

ENCOUNTERING CHALLENGES

NOTE:

This next section may be a difficult one for new leaders to digest because the issues are weighty and may seem overwhelming at first. If the issues don't seem relevant to you right now, simply make a note of them so that you can refer back to them when they are eventually encountered.

For those who have been involved in ministry for some time and have already faced these issues, this section will be immediately useful.

All of us, sooner or later, will have to deal with these matters. But we can have confidence in the midst of it that God will give us the wisdom to act with passion and grace—never expecting us to be perfect, just obedient.

Chapter Ten

MAINTAINING A DEEP SENSE OF COMMUNITY

But if anyone causes one of these
little ones who believe in me to sin,
it would be better for him to have
a large millstone hung around his neck
and to be drowned in the depths of the sea.
Matthew 18:6

God may expand our territories, bringing vast resources and personnel within our spheres of influence, causing our churches or organizations to grow rapidly. Within the increased complexity of our organizational structure, what must we remember from the days of staff intimacy when we all labored side by side? How can we retain a meaningful and strong sense of community?

GOD'S MESSAGE

A few years ago I was invited to give a staff-training seminar for a large, international para-church ministry. On the day of the seminar, I awakened full of excitement, delighted at the prospect of addressing these precious men and women with whom I could identify so easily. Already I felt deeply connected to them. My notes and overheads were packed and waiting in my briefcase by the front door, and I couldn't wait to get going.

Approaching the onramp to the expressway that would take me to the ministry site, I asked God one more time to show me clearly the hearts of those I would be addressing at the seminar. What were their needs and how could I put a laser focus to my teaching in order to best tailor it to their situation? I was surprised by what followed.

While waiting for His answer, an overwhelming sorrow engulfed me! And then the tears came—great tears of pain and confusion that made driving impossible. I eased the car off the highway and came to a stop. God was somehow letting me experience vicariously what they kept hidden day after day. As I bent over the steering wheel weeping, I pleaded with God to tell me what to say to them.

The answer came quickly and gently, "Tell them for Me, '*I hear your cry.*' "

THEIR RESPONSE

I managed to regain my composure and arrived at the ministry a short time later. As I stepped up to the podium, I was engulfed again by the memory of God's message. Leaning forward and adjusting the microphone, I simply but earnestly told them what I had experienced that morning—the sorrow, the tears and God's answer: "*I hear your cry.*"

Immediately, all over that auditorium, the polite smiles of many dissolved into tears as God's love allowed them to be real about the long-standing pain, disappointment and bitterness they had been experiencing because of distant, detached leadership. As I prayed aloud for His healing and guidance for the hours of instruction ahead, the Holy Spirit opened their hearts to forgive and created within them the desire to learn a new way to do ministry within their own spheres of influence.

A COMMON PROBLEM

The larger the ministry, the more separated we as leaders can become from our staff who are giving their lives to make our visions come to pass. It is altogether too easy to be consumed with producing and funding a *project*—while the nurturing of all levels of staff is increasingly neglected. We may find ourselves conducting impersonal meetings in which our major focus is to challenge and motivate them to work harder and be more committed. If our communication is typically only top down and one-sided, resentment and frustration will be rampant among staff in every department.

Wide gaps can develop between us, as visionaries, and those who increasingly feel as though they are little more than numbers on a chart to us. When personal contact between executives and staff is almost non-existent, changes in structure and focus catch them by surprise, leaving them feeling very insecure. Some staff may even fear that they have become a means to an end, dispensable when their strength is spent or they make a mistake. Whether this is true or not, the unaddressed suspicions breed fear and insecurity among the weak, and posturing for power and position among the strong.

Managers and staff who don't feel *valued* for who they are, but only for what they can produce to make our causes succeed, may become cynical and lose the passion they once had for ministry. This is truly tragic. For this we are responsible.

WHEN WE FAIL

If we become autocratic–if we lead by edict rather than by soliciting innovations and insights–we need to repent and apologize, asking them for forgiveness. Communication is the basis of authentic community and must flow between all areas of the ministry. We need others' input, and they need to continually connect with the vision. We must not forget that their lives are just as much invested in the ministry as ours and must be valued. Their having input integrates them with the vision and helps them own it. They consequently not only respect us more, but also feel more dedicated to and responsible for success.

If we travel away from the ministry frequently, we may need someone, particularly with the spiritual gift of administration, to be the conduit between us and our staff. An administrator who understands that his or her gift is to draw everyone into the process of the mission, and will help them reach their individual goals, is invaluable. The administrator can keep communication flowing between us and the rest of our staff while we are on the road, and can be the glue holding us all in the mission together. Best of all, this person will provide the breathing room we need to be able to see the big picture and not get bogged down in details.

ADJUSTED LEADERSHIP PARADIGM

In order for us as visionaries to make an enduring impact on the world for Christ in the 21st century, we will wisely avoid an independent style of leadership and the elitist tendency of the hierarchal system that has prevailed in the past. It's time to bring an honest sense of community to the ministry, no matter how large that ministry has come to be. Order and spiritual authority are necessary, but there must also be mutual respect and understanding—as well as accountability—throughout the ministry, and we are the ones to set that precedent. The ministry has to be a "safe" place for everyone.

GREATER EXPECTATIONS

Followers today seek to be connected deeply to their leaders and the cause, and they expect to be part of the process. They want to understand and own the vision. They also expect to be mentored, coached and given an opportunity to reach their fullest potential.

I can't say this often enough: No longer can we simply assign tasks; we must *develop people*. They know their gifts are indispensable to achieving the goals and they want to be heard, appreciated, trained and empowered to operate at their best. Together, committed to each other and the mission, we can conceive an appropriate process, bring loving correction to the course, cheer one another on to success and celebrate together each victory.

If we as leaders do not first of all learn how to *build community* with and among our people, we will only be *pushing* or *pulling* them toward our vision—often against their will—rather than *leading* them anywhere. It is not enough for the vision to belong to us, or even to the organization, but it must belong to the entire ministry community—owned and cared about by all. We will fail if we are emotionally isolated leaders who avoid vulnerability and refuse to build sincere relationships with our people. The journey must be made together, or it won't be made at all.

TO BUILD COMMUNITY:

1. Be intent upon initiating and sustaining meaningful relationships with others on our ministry staff.
2. Interact with others freely and regularly, hearing "their stories," inviting them to ask honest questions and giving them honest answers.
3. Surrender our need to always be right and seek to learn from others.
4. Don't wait for those with whom we labor to be perfect before investing time and energy in developing their potential.
5. Cheer one another on daily, sharing one another's burdens.
6. Make sure they have an open invitation to speak to us.
7. Risk trusting others while being trustworthy ourselves.
8. Never ask of others what we are unwilling to do ourselves.
9. Listen more than talk.
10. Take responsibility for the spiritual health of our organization.

As we focus as much on instilling a deep sense of community as on fulfilling a dream or vision, others are reassured that we value them, and they will follow our lead gladly.

WITH THOSE CLOSEST TO US

Especially with our leadership team, there must be a powerful bond of respect and love. Respect for each individual will prevent cliques from developing. Getting away together, whether for a few hours or periodic retreats of several days' duration, keeps us real. When the focus on ministry is set aside and we concentrate on enjoying each other's company, we see sides of one another that enable us to identify with and understand each other perhaps for the first time. As we pray together for each other's lives and personal concerns, we learn to care deeply.

Trust grows and we find ourselves willing to sacrifice for one another both inside and outside the ministry workplace. Defensiveness and territorialism take a back seat to growth and flexibility when we know we are loved and valued.

THROUGHOUT THE MINISTRY

As we engender a network of mutual respect, trust and devotion to not only God's plan, but also to all those who have chosen to join us in the cause, the strength and effectiveness of our ministry will grow greatly. As we care for and protect one another in the heat of service, God's grace and power will be released.

DISCUSSION PROBES:

1. Describe what you have observed in a ministry that had forgotten to care for its "lowest level" of workers.
   - What was their greatest hurt?
   - What was their greatest desire?
2. Do you feel alone at the top?
   - Have you lost touch with the grassroots workers or the volunteers that make ministry "happen?'
3. How effective are you at casting vision in a way that communicates everyone's individual importance?
   - What techniques will you develop to do this better?
4. If you have lost touch with your people due to extensive travel, what will you do to heal this breach and prevent communication breakdown in the future?
5. Do you honestly value each worker's life as much as your own?
   - Why or why not?
   - Is there an attitude of which you need to repent?
6. How can you personally let your people know afresh how greatly you value them?
7. How can you periodically honor them in a special way?
   - When will you instate this practice?
8. Have you taken the time recently to get feedback from all levels of the ministry as to ways you could improve communication with them?
   - If not, decide now how to get that feedback as soon as possible.
9. How much time are you spending developing people, as opposed to giving them tasks?
   - If development has been weak, begin now—through seminars, personal meetings, mentoring and by disseminating relevant information on specific subjects. Be creative and systematic.
10. If there is someone on your ministry team with whom you have a strained relationship, resolve it right away!
    - If there is something for which you need to apologize to

your entire organization, team or congregation, do so as soon as possible.

Chapter Eleven

UNDERSTANDING
REACTIONS
TO CONFLICT

See to it that no one messes the grace of
God and that no bitter root grows up
to cause trouble and defile many.
Hebrews 12:15

Among leaders and followers alike, conflict within ministries is not unusual. Wherever there are people, there will be occasion for offending and taking offense, even if only by being different. Too often, however, serious offenses are overlooked until there is either an explosion over something insignificant, or slow alienation which sows distrust and weakens everyone's effectiveness.

Why is it so hard to go to the root of a problem when we first sense it? *Why* do we instead employ one of the following:

1. *Intimidation*: Being tough or distant; controlling by withholding praise; dismissing staff without allowing a discussion or an appeal
2. *Compensation and compliance*: Turning ourselves inside out to please others in the hope of bringing peace
3. *Character assassination or triangulation*: Undermining others' trust of them by talking negatively about them behind their backs, disclosing their faults often in an exaggerated way
4. *Avoidance or isolation*: Pretending everything is all right; purposely fleeing the person or problem; living in emotional isolation

FEAR

I am convinced that an overwhelming number of women respond to conflict through the lens of fear and insecurity. Whether because of having suffered through abusive relationships in the past, or because of being uncertain of our value before God, we are frightened at the prospect of facing conflict. However, to quote a famous movie character—Yoda of *Star Wars* fame—"Fear leads to anger, anger leads to hate, and hate leads to suffering." Fear is no small enemy.

The first step in learning how to resolve conflict positively is understanding that of which we are afraid, and our universal need for healing.

INTIMIDATION

Years ago, I met Barbara, a very powerful woman preacher and para-church ministry founder who had persevered through great opposition in following the call of God on her life. However, while many were impressed with her command of the Word, the anointing upon her preaching and her tireless labor in the ministry, her staff saw her as a somewhat heartless individual.

ROOTS OF HER LIFE

While Barbara was growing up, her parents rarely talked about their feelings and had given her the distinct impression that showing one's feelings was a great sign of weakness. They had weathered the Great Depression through sheer force of will, and expected the same of her when facing difficulty. Consequently, Barbara learned early to forge ahead, never giving in to others' feelings—and repressing her own.

After years of denying her emotional side and focusing instead on the expedient, productive and logical thing—and demanding the same from others—her relationships became stern and sterile. Her life was above reproach, but her staff was intimidated by her forcefulness and just tried to stay out of her way. When there were problems of behavior among them, no one dared appeal to her for mercy. Her answer to conflict was to swiftly dismiss them from the ministry.

Fortunately, God brought a crisis so large into her life that she fell apart and sought counseling. The counselor first took her back in prayer to revisit childhood memories. As each painful scene came before her, she forgave her parents for their harshness with her and then repented of her bitter root judgment against them, breaking the power of intimidation in her life. (See Heb. 12:15 and Matt. 7:1-2) Finally, she asked Jesus to reveal to her heart His tenderness and love for her. As she sensed His loving embrace, she was set free from her fear of being weak or vulnerable. She gratefully came to the realization that Jesus had been tenderly holding her during those dark days. She rejoiced in tears that He understood and received her pain, and that He loved her and was giving her a new heart.

Barbara discovered that God forgave easily when she simply said she was sorry. Her entire countenance softened and her heart became very tender toward those who were hurting. She set about changing the way in which she led in her ministry.

She began again with her staff—inviting them to express their feelings about the ministry and letting them give input into solving the problems that surfaced from then on. This previously tough, unapproachable lady asked for their forgiveness.

She encouraged each of them to receive inner healing counseling as well, so that they would all be free to be honest with each other and not hide conflict from her. The ministry today is healthy, loving and growing in God's blessing. Truth has triumphed and dispelled the fear under which they had been laboring.

IF THIS IS YOU

If you find yourself leading others by intimidation, it may be that you are afraid of losing control by showing your heart. If you have had to fend for yourself all through life, you will cover your insecurities by coming on strong and dominating a situation. To you, sensitivity equals weakness—weakness that invited danger in the heartless world in which you grew up. Therefore, you now lead by tight control of those under your authority, not realizing that vulnerability would actually strengthen your leadership.

One of the worst results of your denying your own feelings and hiding behind a façade of toughness and total competence is that others are made to feel weak in contrast. Those who are less secure feel devalued and judged, afraid to approach you with the constructive criticism and wisdom you need from them—and you all lose.

Seek Christian counseling for your fears, and repent of any judgments you may have made against yourself or others. Pray for the joy, sensitivity and confidence of Christ to flood your heart each day.

COMPENSATION

In the past, I found myself at the other end of the spectrum from Barbara. My perception of life and ministry was wrapped up in feelings. On the positive side, my sensitivity to pain and others' needs made it easy for me to respond to the call to teach at Teen Challenge, a ministry full of broken lives. Because of my tenderness and compassion, students were more quickly able to believe that God loved and forgave them. The Holy Spirit often brought emotional healing to their lives during my classes.

The downside was that, in the early days, I bent over backward to please others whenever there was conflict. Even if someone else was at fault, I'd blame myself, beating myself up. Dismissing someone from my department was almost impossible; I was afraid to confront because I feared that all *my* own faults would be exposed. How could I confront when I myself wasn't perfect? Besides, what if they got angry or violent?

ROOTS OF MY LIFE

I was raised in a supportive, Christian home by loving parents who expected me to be an exemplary daughter. When I did well, I was profusely praised; when I disappointed them, the message I received was that everyone in the community was watching and that my witness for Christ had been damaged. I grew up feeling personally responsible to protect God's image by walking very circumspectly. It was as though the whole world were watching, and I'd better not mess up!

I hungered for a God who would defend me, who would love me even if I didn't do everything right.

THE RESULT

To be healthy and successful as a leader, I had to forgive my parents for emphasizing my "testimony" to the world over my personal value to God, and I had to embrace God's forgiveness for my inadequacies and sins. As I did, I began to sense God's complete acceptance—whether I played the role right or not! I realized then that God wasn't as concerned about what I did to His reputation, as He was that I remain authentic in my relationship with Him and others.

I have finally come to see conflict as an opportunity to refine my love for others and deepen those relationships as I value them—just as I desire to be valued. This allows truth to triumph. I know now that I will not be of more—or less—value no matter who is proven more right.

CHARACTER ASSASSINATION OR TRIANGULATION

Many women have developed an insidious substitute for confrontation—undermining one another verbally behind each other's backs. It's amazing that while our gender is gifted with a tremendous ability to communicate life verbally, we sometimes use that ability to destroy one another!

If you have ever led a women's ministry, you know how often vision and passion can be destroyed by backbiting and two-faced behavior. To your face they affirm your leadership—and even try to ingratiate themselves to you in an attempt to gain personal power—and then privately criticize everything about you to other women in the ministry. A women's ministry director in a large church recently told me that triangulation—not going straight to the offender, but rather talking negatively about her to others—has been the biggest deterrent to success in that ministry.

REBELLION

This scenario reminds me of Absolom's undermining of his father, King David. Absolom, who had access to the palace and was privy to leadership policy, proceeded to prompt others—who had been previously content—to criticize David, appearing to be the people's champion. He encouraged grievances, blowing them out of proportion, gaining the position of "defender of right" by subtly undermining truth. He never actually wanted a better government. If he had, he could have approached his father and helped bring any change that might have been needed. In his heart Absolom had judged David, and his revenge was to overthrow his father and then take his place on the throne.

TODAY

There will be those under your leadership who have made bitter root judgments in their hearts that have nothing to do with you. That bitterness will cause them to be constant inciters of rebellion, if only by gossiping behind your back, casting doubt on your leadership ability. They are after power at your expense, yet they would have no idea how to do your job. Bitterness and the pain of unhealed wounds inflicted by past authority figures drive them, and they bolster their own sense of worth by undermining yours. You need to recognize it for what it is and gently, but firmly, address it. (Chapter Ten discusses how to do this.)

AVOIDANCE OR ISOLATION

Women who isolate themselves after fear enters their hearts during a conflict may not really believe that God loves them or that they are worthy of justice. Perhaps they have experienced what they consider a major failure in their lives and are ashamed to be well known. Perhaps they have been told at some time that they are worthless!

On the outside, they appear to be gentle souls who are unassuming and very humble. But inside there is a raging fire set by the fear of losing what little bit of self-worth and dignity they feel they still have. In isolation, they nurse their hurts and sink deeper into secret despondency. They may fear being hurt further if they are honest about their feelings. Perhaps people would reject them altogether if they knew how weak their fear has made them. How desperately they need to receive faithful, unconditional love!

Such women don't always hide themselves from participating in ministry; they might be very gifted and quite visible. But they have very few, if any, close friends. They may be cheerful and engaging with everyone on Sunday, but absolutely alone during the week. They are sweetly passive in a group, and if given responsibility, will procrastinate until it's nearly too late to act. They struggle to believe that they can truly succeed at anything. When someone even comes close to trying to correct them, they run as fast as they can from the scene and dodge that person from then on. They expose to no one the resentment and sense of failure that consume them.

OUR PATTERNS

It seems as though *leaders* are generally more susceptible to reacting to conflict with intimidation or compensation; *followers*, with triangulation and avoidance. However, the same route to wholeness is required of all. Because emotional healing is so needed in the body of Christ, we must be sure that our ministries are training those gifted in compassion and exhortation, and faithful on their knees, to pray others through to victory and then help them learn to walk in it.

All of us have sinned, and all of us have been sinned against. The fears that arise from carrying the pain alone are many: of rejection, being proven wrong, losing face, failure, abandonment, vulnerability and exposure, and losing control. Anger, degrees of hatred—especially self-hatred—and suffering accompany all of them. The cure will come when we carry one another in prayer into the arms of God, helping one another forgive, repent and believe.

DISCUSSION PROBES:

1. When you are unsure of your authority, which reaction is easiest for you?
   a) Intimidation
   b) Compensation or compliance
   c) Character assassination or triangulation
   d) Avoidance or isolation
   - Why?
2. List your most common fears as a leader. Be brutally honest.
3. What from your past encouraged these fears?
   - When were you most wounded by an authority figure?
   - Whom must you forgive?
   - Of what judgments against them must you repent so as not to transfer those judgments onto others who remind you of them?
4. Describe a crisis situation where you, as a leader, were sucked into responding improperly.
   - Is there someone to whom you have not apologized?
   - Whom must you forgive?
5. Think of different examples of women within your sphere of influence who typically model any of these four responses to conflict.
   - In what ways do you understand them better since reading this chapter?
6. Develop a plan to dialog with your ministry workers, small group leaders, or council about these responses. Help them discover their own weaknesses and begin the process of healing and redirection.
7. Go to a leader whom you feel responds creatively and biblically to conflict. Ask him or her to explain his or her process of thinking, feeling and acting during different kinds of conflict.
8. Which causes you more pain—attacks on your character or on your leadership plan and abilities?
   - Why?
9. Where do you go when you are afraid?

- Who comforts and reaffirms you?
- List some of the scriptures that help restore your courage.
10. Describe three roles of the Holy Spirit in helping you develop a healthy leadership model during conflict.

Chapter Twelve

RESOLVING CONFLICT MEANINGFULLY

And the Lord's servant must not quarrel; instead,
he must be kind to everyone, able to teach, not resentful.
Those who oppose him he must gently instruct,
in the hope that God will grant them repentance
leading them to a knowledge of the truth...
II Timothy 2:24, 25a

I have often heard it said that conflict is a blessing—that it reveals dangerous weaknesses in the ministry—and that resolution brings growth to all involved. Conflict reveals issues that not only separate us from each other, but also separate us from God. Furthermore, our character is refined in its fire. God uses our discomfort with it to expose our fears, pride and prejudices. The only true failure comes in not bringing it to a resolution. But even then, we can learn from it.

While this is absolutely true, it is no fun being in the middle of a volatile situation! However, the *absence* of conflict is even worse. Experiencing *no* conflict can mean that there is no passion or energy for the work at hand, that we haven't captured their hearts with the vision, or that we have been too domineering, leaving no room for their creativity and diversity. They have simply shut down in boredom or hopelessness.

FACING CONFLICT

Unlike conflict that arises from bitterness and requires inner healing, conflict that arises from our differences can usually be resolved rather quickly. In fact, *most* conflict stems from misunderstandings which can be easily cleared up through listening to one another. Our underlying desire must be to find truth and bring peace and growth to all involved.

When facing conflict, we must know that we are of great value to God, but that our value doesn't come from being right all the time. We must also be assured that while it is true that we will be able to discern *others'* failings, we too will fail and need correction, healing and accountability!

DEALING WITH THOSE UNDER OUR AUTHORITY

Before we can successfully address any difficulties in the ministry, we must have made it possible for others to trust us. Our effectiveness depends upon the trust level we have established, and whether we have placed high value on them. When they feel safe with us and trust us, they will more easily hear us and be open to correction.

To build trust, we must:

1. Be authentic
   a. Be transparent (no hypocrisy; no hiding of our own weaknesses)
   b Remain vulnerable (willing to get close enough to risk

being hurt)
2. Honor them
   a. Encourage them; listen to them
   b. Invest in their success
   c. Keep our word; be consistent in word and deed; don't let walls of silence build
   d. Keep confidences (remember that their story is not ours to tell)

When we meet with a member of our ministry who has become disgruntled or is stirring up dissension, for instance, it is wise to first encourage their true strengths, letting them know that we value them. Then we can simply ask permission to share what we see that could be improved. We should stick to a discussion of the specific problem, not bringing up past failures, and be direct and non-threatening.

As we listen carefully to their responses, we can begin asking questions to help them evaluate the problem for themselves, and together we can decide on a course of action to make things right or to clear the air. If they have grievances against us personally, we need to hear their grievances and consider them carefully. If we need to apologize, we must do so immediately and fully. If they ask forgiveness for their offenses, we can forgive generously and assure them that it will go no further.

In closing the session, we should pray with them, instilling hope for the future. In a few days, it would be wise to follow up with them, renewing our commitment to their success. It is amazing how quickly they will respond to our efforts to resolve differences. It shows that we care—that we value them and our relationship with them.

AN ILLUSTRATION

About a year ago, Mary, a friend of mine, began serving as Business Administrator at a large denominational church, with about ten employees reporting to her. One of these employees was Sue, a woman who delighted in pushing the envelope—coming in late, working at odd times when the building should have been closed, getting involved in operations that she hadn't been hired to do and wasting time chatting from office to office. Her attitude was that if her authorities gave her a hassle, she'd simply walk away from the job and the church. She was *not* going to have anyone telling her how to do her job! She thought she had everyone over a barrel because she alone had the skill for the work she performed. Besides, she had gotten away with her independence for quite some time. She was a formidable woman whom no one had dared cross. Privately, the pastors and all the secretaries wanted Sue to be fired.

After beginning the job, Mary slowly built a relationship with Sue, observing carefully all Sue's activities first hand. Then Mary called Sue into her office and shut the door. She surprised Sue by first complimenting her on the quality of her work, citing specific examples. Mary assured Sue that she was a great asset to the staff, but that there were some matters that concerned her.

This wise leader then simply and concisely—without judgment or personal comment—listed the unacceptable behaviors. Sue, expecting to be fired, stiffened and began planning her exit.

But she was arrested by Mary's next comment: "I want to work with you. I want to help you become the best employee we have. I want you to have the joy of complete success in this job. But you must know that your past independence cannot continue."

Since Sue hadn't walked out, Mary took it as a sign to proceed, and outlined a plan. She said that they would take it one day at a time and reevaluate Sue's progress each Friday for one month. If there was improvement, they'd continue working together for another month, with continued regular accountability checkups during that time. If, at the end of three months Mary felt that they had been successful in turning the situation around, she would love to have Sue stay on in her present position, with an opportunity for a promotion later. If they hadn't been successful, she would sadly have to let Sue go. It was that simple.

Sue was stunned by how thoroughly Mary had planned out the process and by Mary's evident desire to see her succeed. When Mary began to pray for her, asking God to bless her as she became obedient, there were actually tears in this "tough" lady's eyes. Her heart had been won by someone who cared enough about her to stop her from destroying her future, and to walk with her through to success.

They followed the plan exactly as Mary had prescribed. On Fridays, Mary evaluated her progress and mentored her, and during the week, Mary went out of her way to encourage her. Everyone on staff was amazed at the energy and attention to guidelines Sue suddenly brought to her job.

OUR EXPECTATIONS

I believe that people rise—or sink—to the level of our expectations. If we want them to rise, we must be ready to provide mentoring and accountability so that their success can be measured and obvious, especially to them. Edicts alone never change behavior; *an investment in their lives*—carefully planned, measurable and within healthy boundaries—brings amazing results.

If they resist our efforts and only become more troublesome, we will need to return to the line we drew in the sand, which has obviously been crossed, bringing separation for the sake of everyone. Unfortunately, they have a free will, and even the best intervention can be rejected. Sometimes a person doesn't get serious about straightening out until they hit bottom. We need to know when to let that happen and not feel guilty about letting them go.

WITH WOMEN SERVING WITH US IN OUR MINISTRY

Most of us are not in an employer's position of authority over the women who cause us grief in the ministry. We cannot fire them. While the principles of resolving conflict are similar, it will take more personal courage to confront them.

I have found that, after an offense, it is critical that I take the time to get beyond my hurt feelings or embarrassment to discern the reason for the attack. Had it been a simple misunderstanding? Or was she just having a rotten day, for which she would probably apologize to me later? Had I been thoughtless toward her or had I just gotten caught in the crossfire of her anger at someone else? Is now the time to speak to her, or might it resolve itself if I simply show her kindness?

When confrontation *is* necessary, I find it helpful to *first determine the goals she and I have in common, and how alienation is undermining reaching those goals.* Rather than pitting us against ourselves, I seek to show her how the enemy is trying to keep us both from glorifying God. As I take this approach, I too am free to hear any hard truth about myself that she gives me when I invite her to share her feelings. We find ourselves on the same side of the conflict, with a common enemy, rather than shooting at each other as Satan would like.

AN ILLUSTRATION

A few years ago, a woman, who served in the same church ministry as I, misunderstood something that I said in a meeting and began talking negatively behind my back. I was totally caught off guard. I was truly innocent of what she was accusing me.

At first, my reaction to her unwarranted criticism of me was to ignore it and let my integrity be my protection. However, as she continued to undermine my authority as a teacher and leader, I found myself constantly fatigued and wanting to quit the ministry— my energy spent and my joy gone. It suddenly dawned on me that Satan was having a great time using these dynamics.

Prompted by a friend, I prepared to address the situation. As soon as I had come to the place where I could weep for her instead of myself, and grieve over the damage to the ministry—rather than over my hurt feelings—I knew I could go in love and speak to her from my heart. It was a powerful learning experience for me.

By the grace of God, I was able to speak gently with her, face to face, and draw a picture of what had happened. She saw how her accusations and demeaning remarks spoken in secret behind my back had grieved the Holy Sprit and had hurt her own position of authority as well. Her heart broke with mine over the terrible example that triangulation—talking negatively to others rather than coming directly to me for resolution—had been to the younger women who looked up to us. In tears she asked my forgiveness and we wept together. Our next task was to sincerely honor one another before the other women, and model restoration.

A few weeks later, I was surprised to see that she was still not at rest. I discovered that she was having a terrible time forgiving herself! I assured her that it was *over*, that it was totally forgiven and would *never* be brought up to her again. Finally, she accepted Jesus' death for it and the gift of forgiveness, and let it go.

THE BEAUTY OF MEDIATION

Occasionally, we may find ourselves in conflict with someone who is characteristically bent on having the last word at all cost, or who intimidates us because he/she is strong-willed. With such a person, coming to an equitable resolution will require a mediator.

In choosing a mediator, we must look for a person who is respected by both of us, a person who has perhaps worked with both of us and knows our strengths and weaknesses. This person must be objective, with no reason to side with one or the other of us and be acceptable by both of us.

I have used such a person to bring reconciliation between another woman in ministry and myself when I doubted my ability to stand against her strength of will and get her to hear my heart. First, I contacted her, expressing my sorrow over the breach between us and my desire for resolution and reconciliation. We then agreed upon a mediator, a man with whom we had both served on foreign mission trips in the past.

We met at a neutral location and he opened with prayer. As we each took our turn speaking, he reflected back what he was hearing, making sure we were understanding one another. He also shared insights about each of us that shed light on our reactions to our past experience together. After three hours of sharing, reflecting, apologizing and forgiving, we were restored to one another as friends and fellow laborers for the Gospel's sake. We learned so much in that one session about the intricacies of the strengths and weaknesses of our two very different personalities and the depth of trust and communication that it takes to work as a team in difficult circumstances! We will both be better leaders because of the wisdom gained that day. Perhaps what we learned during that brief afternoon was worth the pain of the initial conflict!

BASIC BENEFITS

Having a mediator creates a safe place for both parties. We can be relaxed and think more clearly as the mediator keeps the discussion balanced and prevents it from being dominated or controlled by either of us. It is the mediator who keeps us fixed on the ultimate goals—understanding and valuing one another, forgiving, spiritual and emotional growth, as well as a fresh start in a relationship worth saving.

TO BRING RESOLUTION:

1. Pray and take time to get God's perspective
2. Search our hearts for any offense we might have given
3. Try to forgive before approaching them
4. Look for the reason we both want it resolved
5. Speak face to face to avoid giving the wrong message
6. Encourage and empower them to speak first
7. Listen thoughtfully; ask questions for understanding; reflect back to them for clarity
8. Don't be defensive when they speak. It's the issue that's in question, not our value.
9. If new information is revealed, don't rush. It may be wise to take more time to evaluate. (We may need more than one meeting.)
10. If attacked, listen for the source of the hurt
11. Ask to speak and then state our side truthfully
    a. Own our feelings
    b. State our views as perceptions that could be wrong
    c. Stick to the present issue; don't make a personality or character judgment; don't bring up the past
    d. Be teachable
    e. Be the first to own our own sin and ask forgiveness, even if it is miniscule compared to theirs! Release any expectation of receiving an apology
    f. Desire to change; be part of the solution
    g. Be grateful for their openness

14. If they apologize, accept the apology graciously
15. Pray together
16. Follow up as reinforcement of the fresh start

Again, this may be much easier to do in the presence of a mediator, especially if the issues are serious and emotions run deep. How wonderful it would be if every ministry had mature individuals who were trained in the art of mediation upon whom we could call! What an invaluable resource they would be for the body of Christ!

As leaders, if we haven't already, we should learn how to mediate and should provide training for those in our ministry who desire to serve the body as mediators.

WITH THOSE OVER US

A third situation in which we may find ourselves is when our authorities sin or act unethically, and God calls us to address it. This is not as difficult as it might seem, if we know who we are in Christ.

Bill Gothard, in his Basic Youth Conflicts Seminar, describes it as "Making an appeal with a right heart." What he means is to first:

1. Forgive, leaving judgment to God (If we have not forgiven, they will sense our judgment, be defensive and not hear a word of our appeal)
2. Go to the person with a respectful attitude, asking permission to share a concern
3. Express it as something that could deeply hurt the leader's ministry or integrity—not as a personal accusation
4. Appeal to them to seek God's view of it
5. Leave the matter with them, assuring them that we will not talk about it with anyone else, but will instead be praying for them to have the courage to act upon whatever the Holy Spirit may reveal to them

VARYING EXPERIENCES

I personally followed these steps with a former pastor on two occasions and, because of the trust that had already existed between us, I was truly heard. On one of the issues, he immediately repented. On the other, he said he would pray about it. Regardless, I was free as soon as I had given my appeal and put the results into God's hands. *I was not his judge—only a fellow warrior who wanted his safety and success.*

But it doesn't always work so neatly. If your authority leads by intimidation, for instance, he or she will probably not grant you a hearing if they suspect that you question their behavior. The roots of their defensiveness and the reasons for their power tactics are most often buried deep within childhood fears of loss of control or because they are bound by perfectionism. Until they are healed in heart, they will not hear criticism without retaliating.

Know your limits in addressing them. Spend time on your knees and be assured that God will let their behavior go only so far before allowing them to utterly fail. In brokenness alone will they seek healing of heart and repent. Surrender to God all your expectations of them for the present and release them to the only One Who can change their hearts.

WHEN WE ARE CONFRONTED
BY OUR AUTHORITIES, WE NEED TO:

1. Listen carefully, without argument
2. Reflect back to them what we are hearing, to make sure we understand the problem.
3. Resist reacting emotionally or taking it as a judgment of our personal value.
4. Be unafraid and state our perceptions simply.
5. Resist launching a counterattack. Stick to the issue at hand.
6. If it becomes evident that we were indeed wrong, repent, naming the offense.
7. Receive any discipline gratefully, knowing that a clean heart will last much longer in the ministry than a wounded ego.
8. If we were not wrong, rest in our own innocence, knowing that God sees and will set things straight in His time.
9. If necessary, ask for a mediator, if the charges are serious

and untrue. .

DON'T TAKE OFFENSE

Unfortunately, our leaders may use disappointing methods when they try to talk to us about a problem. We need to recognize that many factors may be playing into the crisis, including the pressures they are under and their possible discomfort with confronting, causing them to do so poorly.

The truth is that most ministry leaders have not been trained in constructive confrontation or conflict resolution. They simply don't know how to do it. Look beyond their handling of it to what God has for you to learn. Listen to the Holy Spirit as you try to hear their heart. At the very least, we can learn how *not* to confront those under our own leadership. Whatever we do, we must not make a bitter root judgment against our authority, for that judgment will truly defile us and others.

A COMMON BLUNDER

Sometimes a leader will challenge or confront someone under their authority using information given them by someone who has triangulated a personal issue by complaining to the leader. Often, leaders get trapped into thinking that they must solve these conflicts rather than send the accuser back to the alleged offender. The only obligation the leader *actually* has in such a situation is to help the accuser deal with his or her own fear of confronting, and perhaps offer to be a mediator if one becomes necessary.

OUR NEED TO GIVE HONOR

Above all, we must honor our authorities at all times. God has given them to us for our safety and instruction, and He will use them for our good whether they are always wise or not. In fact, God often uses unfair authorities to reveal and deal with our own pride or impatience! It's amazing how God can use someone else's irrational, immature or offensive behavior to make us into His image. Through it all, He has His eye on *our* spiritual growth and behavior...and He loves us dearly. If conditions become oppressive, God will lead us out. Meanwhile, we must guard our hearts and ask Him to purify our responses!

REVIEW:

1. Our personal lives affect our ministry. Most, if not all of us, need inner healing from the pains and sins of our pasts.
2. We *will* make mistakes, but we can grow through them.
3. It is wise to move early on a problem, not allowing it to fester out of fear.
4. Our views are very valuable and we must not be afraid to voice them. *How* we voice them can make all the difference.
5. Before appealing to anyone for resolution, we must forgive. If we don't, our unforgiveness will cause them to be defensive. They will focus on our attitude and miss the point.
6. We must know when to cease appealing to an authority for change, leaving the results to God.
7. It is critical to honor and value others, especially our leaders, at all times.
8. Those under us are watching and learning from our example.
9. When we are wrong and must change, we must not take it as a judgment against our value as a person. It does not diminish God's love for us.
10. We will grow by inviting correction.
11. It is not our business to pick up others' offenses.
12. Using a mediator is a life-saver when emotions and issues run deep, or when one party is likely to dominate the other.
13. Irritating people are sometimes used to reveal our pride or impatience.
14. Conflict that exists simply because of differences in opinion can actually stimulate creativity.
15. We need to embrace discipline, even if it seems to be more than we deserve. God will use it in more ways than we can

imagine!

16. God is in control.

AND FINALLY...

Blessed are the Peacemakers: those who will walk with others through the valley of growth; those who desire truth more than personal victory; and those ready to repent, forgive and love again.

DISCUSSION PROBES:

1. List three benefits of your associates having different view-points and perceptions on any given issue.
2. What are you doing to build trusting relationships with those with whom you minister?
   - Why is trust so critical?
   - Name three ways in which trust can easily be destroyed.
3. In the past, how difficult has it been for you to take correction?
   - Has the age or sex of the person correcting you made a difference in how well you have handled it?
4. Describe a time someone used great tact and love while addressing you with a grievance.
   - Give a contrasting example of when someone addressed you in a very hurtful way.
5. Why is triangulation so difficult to deal with?
   - Have you ever been guilty of it yourself?
   - What were the negative consequences?
   - How will you respond when someone under your authority "tells on" someone else to you rather than going directly to the offender?
6. Re-read the story in this chapter about Mary and Sue.
   - If Sue had been a volunteer instead of an employee, how would Mary's approach have been different?
   - How would it have been the same?
7. Think of a problem individual in your own ministry and then apply the advice, "First, determine the goals he/she and I have in common, and how alienation is undermining reaching those goals."
   - What are his/her ministry goals?
   - How can you help him/her see the damage being done to those goals by his/her improper or irresponsible behavior?
   - As you look at it from his/her perspective, are you able to be more objective and compassionate?
8. Think of a time at which you handled conflict poorly.
   - Have you forgiven yourself?

- Have you forgiven others involved?
- Do you desire to see them blessed—or cursed?

9. In mediation, why is it important that the mediator reflect back to each party what he/she thinks was said?
    - Choose a conflict common to your ministry setting and, with a mediator, role play resolution.

10. Do you still have wounds from a previous ministry situation, especially given by an authority figure?
    - How could it have been resolved with what information you know now?
    - What can you do to be sure that the fear of its happening again won't hamstring you if you face something similar again?

Chapter Thirteen

THE ROLE OF GRACE
IN RESOLVING
CONFLICT

*Blessed is he whose transgressions are forgiven,
whose sins are covered. Blessed is the man
whose sin the Lord does not count against him
and in whose spirit is no deceit.*
Psalm 32:1, 2

In truth, many of us may not *believe* that God really loves us unconditionally. Since the day of our salvation, most of us have been collecting a secret list of laws of proper behavior—laws that we assume we must obey to gain His approval. While we struggle to be worthy, we never quite feel secure, never certain we have the validity to act on God's word and expect the promised results. Since it takes confidence and a strong sense of our personal value to God to address conflict rather than intimidate, compensate, verbally assassinate or hide, we have great difficulty bringing true healing into tense situations.

THE HIDDEN STRENGTH OF OUR LIVES

It has taken me twenty-five years in the ministry to come to the place where I have even an inkling of the magnitude of God's grace for my life. Perhaps we all have too narrowly defined the power of Christ's death and resurrection. Instead, we sometimes behave as though the battle were still ours, to be won by our own devices. If only we could understand that "For by grace are you saved..." is *forever!* It truly provides our release from having to be perfect to be loved—inerrant, wise and failure proof—and it enables us to face reality unafraid. The marvelous fact is that we are *constantly* being saved from our old ways by a living relationship with Jesus Christ Who paid the price for every weakness—within us and others— year after year, all the days of our lives.

Our repentance and His ready forgiveness restore us quickly and give us the courage to trust Him to change us...*and* our responses to those around us. When we repent of our pitiful attempts to rescue ourselves—and our demand that others somehow redeem us by changing themselves—we will become free to see and say the truth in hard situations.

The glory of being forgiven causes us to cherish truth so much that others' power to color our views is destroyed, and intimacy with Him ushers in new understanding. Living in love with One who embraces us when all others flee causes us to surrender to His Spirit's work in us no matter what the earthly consequence. When we are wrong, discipline and correction can be embraced without shame, knowing He will carry us through to maturity. As we rest in His unfailing love, others' behavior or judgments of us lose their ability to diminish or destroy us. And when we are wronged and innocent, we discover an amazing reserve of compassion for even the most offensive culprit!

Until we are convinced and deeply convicted of His grace toward us *and* others, we will never be able to behave *justly*. Without grace, victimization on one hand, or control and manipulation on the other, will haunt our responses. We will also be powerless to bring correction and renewal to those within our spheres of influence who offend or are offended.

IN THE PRESENCE OF OUR ENEMIES

As we learn to live by grace, we die to providing our own security. We see Jesus spreading a table filled with all the safety we need—right in the presence of those who we fear would like to destroy us. Out of that safety, we are able to speak lovingly and compassionately to those who offend us or undermine our every move. We finally see that they simply, sadly don't know Him nor do they trust Him. Grace has not arrived for them yet; the law and the need to be "right" still hold them in its grip. Until they are free in the arms of grace, God's dealings in their lives will always be suspect. They will fight the lonely, futile battle of self-preservation—preservation of a "self" that does nothing but keep them in turmoil. *Death* is what we all need—death to performing for approval, being the smartest, or forever being "right." However, if we *resist* trusting God through such a death, intimacy will be forever out of reach.

INTO HIS ARMS

This dying to our old ways of protecting ourselves during conflict can be frightening at first. It resembles the totally powerless sensation of free falling from a cliff high above His invisible arms, trusting that He will catch us. Dying to ourselves will mean that we will not grab at the branches of argument, justification or accusation on the way down, but we will look instead only toward heaven as we fall, everything staked on His Word to us.

We can trust the Father. Jesus has shown us that He will never betray our trust; He will always bless and never curse. Our Father is faithful and kind. His mercy endures forever. He will never leave us nor forsake us; He will forgive us over and over again; and He will give us the wisdom to forgive others even if they never say they are sorry. Furthermore, He will guide us into all truth and teach us by

His Spirit what we could never figure out intellectually. Out of the manifest grace of God comes the confidence to deal honestly, openly and fearlessly with the conflicts we face as we encounter daily a stumbling world and our own ornery flesh.

GRACE MAKES THE DIFFERENCE

Without grace, how awful we can be to one another! How locked into continual pain and insecurity we are when our identity is in what we *try to be* instead of *who we are in Christ!* As we abandon our laws of worthiness and accept His love for us, we will be able to face conflict seeking truth rather than concentrating on self-protection. It *is* possible to truly cast our cares on Him and trust His ways with abandonment as we boldly face what we fear!

When grace has taken hold, and we know how much we are loved by God, we can experience conflict without rancor and address it without being intimidated. Because we have tasted His heart-changing love and forgiveness for ourselves, we are *convinced* that He has the power to change and reconcile hearts. Out of this conviction, we will have the courage to openly address difficult issues and help bring genuine resolution. Our old *reactions* will have changed to loving *responses.*

And grace will own the day.

DISCUSSION PROBES:

1. Describe the role of grace in your becoming a Christian.
   - What does grace mean to you now?
2. As a conscientious believer, are you honestly convinced that God loves you as much when you are wrong as when you are right?
   - Explain your conviction.
3. What is your first reaction when you are misunderstood or wronged by others in the ministry?
4. Describe a conflict situation where you successfully addressed it head on. What was in your heart toward them that facilitated resolution?
   - What was in their heart that caused them to respond favorably?
5. What does this mean: "My integrity will be my protection?"
   - Describe a time when you were wronged and you responded with silence.
   - What was the outcome?
6. What questions do you ask yourself when abuse comes your way?
   - How do you determine the degree of your own contribution to the conflict?
7. Describe a situation where you had to apologize to someone under your leadership.
   - With what emotions and thoughts did you wrestle?
8. What does *death to self* during conflict mean to you?
9. How can a deep understanding of grace—God's unmerited favor—enable you to address conflict with a strong-willed person without being intimidated?
10. Describe a situation where you did everything right in addressing the problem, and your help and correction were resisted.
    - Did your antagonist take revenge? If so, how?
    - How did you respond to the fallout that caused?

Chapter Fourteen

NAVIGATING THE MINEFIELD OF FRIENDSHIP

Two are better than one,
because they have a good return for their work:
If one falls down, his friend can help him up.
Ecclesiastes 4:9, 10

When we are visible leaders in any ministry, relationships with those around us become more challenging. We may find ourselves beleaguered by the unrealistic expectations of some, and vulnerable as well to being "used" by others who hope to gain importance through association. Their betraying our trust is also a danger. How can we navigate such minefields and remain lovingly connected to those ministering with us or under our leadership?

A COMMON SCENARIO

On a chilly November evening, my husband and I drove two hours through the drizzling rain to a ministry leaders' prayer meeting where several dear friends from various churches in the area were gathering. We had trouble finding the host church and arrived late.

As we slipped into our seats, we heard someone crying. Glancing quickly around the small circle, I saw that the tears were coming from Marcie, a gentle, compassionate woman who co-pastors with her husband, Jack, in a small but growing church in a neighboring town. Struggling to gain her composure, she haltingly began to explain what had happened that had upset her so. Bewildered and wounded—but not bitter—she told her story.

"Mark and Beth, elders in our congregation with whom Jack and I had become close friends, have recently and unexpectedly turned against us. First, Mark voiced criticism of our leadership to the pastor of a neighboring church, with whom he had been spending more and more time. And then, without ever addressing their grievances to us personally, Mark and Beth both ridiculed our leadership style in front of several couples within our own church!

"But worst of all, personal family matters that I had shared in confidence with Beth became public knowledge as Beth used the church grapevine to spread private and sensitive information. I was humiliated by this betrayal at the hands of someone whom I had trusted deeply for several years.

"When we attempted to address the wrongs, Mark and Beth simply resigned and left to attend the neighboring church. So here we are, all still in the same town, but unreconciled. It is almost more than I can bear!" Her last words came out in an agonized whisper.

Jack sat in stone-faced silence as Marcie wept. He was trying to forgive and move on, but in his heart he was saying to God, *Never again, never again will I trust someone close to me in my church.*

Marcie, on the other hand, knew she was on the way to forgiving, even though the pain was fresh. Furthermore, she was determined to remain vulnerable to people in the body; she was willing to risk injury *again* rather than withdraw and isolate herself in the midst of ministry. I was amazed at her willingness to suffer in order to model transparency before the believers under her care.

ANOTHER STORY

At the same time many miles away, Nicole, the Women's Pastor of a growing congregation on the West Coast, was also in for a surprise. An old friend, who had lived at a distance for many years and visited from time to time, had moved into the area. Nicole admittedly had mixed emotions when she heard the news that Beverly would be attending her church.

How will I pastor an old friend? she wondered. The dynamics of the relationship were sure to be different.

When Beverly arrived, she expected their casual, buddy relationship to continue—even grow. She wanted Nicole to shop with her, meet her for lunch often, and be available whenever she called or stopped in at the church office. She fully expected Nicole to be her best friend.

"I tried to explain to Beverly that, between pastoral duties and family responsibilities, I just wouldn't have that kind of free time. I very carefully told Beverly that, with so many other women in the congregation wanting to be my best friend as well, I really couldn't show favoritism to one over another.

"But even more importantly, I knew that God was calling me to distance myself from relationships that would be draining on my energy and time. I was in a season of change and personal spiritual growth, needing first to be refreshed in solitude with God, not absorbed with other people. I didn't know how Beverly would handle all this, but I had to be honest with her.

"Well," Nicole continued, "Beverly couldn't grasp my perspective and felt snubbed. She mistook my 'strange behavior' as rejection and elitism. Somewhere between hurt and anger, Beverly began sowing discord in the body by talking about my 'cruelty and coldness'."

When Nicole and I talked recently, she was *very nearly* at the point of giving up on friendship altogether, sorely tempted to erect permanent walls around her heart and life and let *no one in*, except her family. A very sensitive, caring woman, Nicole felt trapped between anger and cynicism by Beverly's selfishness.

TWO SIDES OF THE STRUGGLE

So then, what is the right way to navigate the difficult terrain of friendships within our ministries? When I am with Marcie, I agree with her that, surely, we must remain vulnerable. Surely the benefits of transparency—others learning from watching our lives, and the joy of having dear friends within our ministries—outweigh the danger of our trust being betrayed someday. How can others learn to be open if we as leaders are not open first? And don't we have needs too for buddies to laugh and cry with who are close by and share our ministry dreams?

Yes, yes!

But when I am with Nicole and see the level of intensity in her prophetic and preaching ministry, I agree with her as well! She needs space from people who pull her away from solitude with God when she finally gets home from the church. She has no time for the distractions of petty jealousies and rivalries for her friendship when she is trying to pastor all the ladies with equal passion.

DIFFERENT LEADERSHIP STYLES

I began to look more closely at the issue of leadership style and discovered that it truly affects the way we enter into friendships. Marcie's leadership style is very pastoral and she thoroughly enjoys mentoring on a personal level. She acts as a mother and sister, creating close, transparent bonds with all who want to learn from her. She will continue to entrust her heart to those who serve and worship in her congregation.

On the other hand, Nicole's leadership style is visionary and prophetic. For her, close friends will be few and will not live close by. She chooses carefully anyone in whom she confides. Trust will have to be earned by others, and even then, the friendships will be held lightly in her hands.

While their approaches are different, they *both* know that close friendships are valuable in bringing comfort and comradeship, as well as in teaching us to care and give of ourselves trustingly. Neither would "use" a friendship to promote herself or exclude others. They are both servants, committed to love those in the body without discrimination.

They also know that they need another's input, another who knows them better than they know themselves and who has earned the right through faithfulness to gently reveal their blind spots so that they won't stumble.

FINDING CLOSE FRIENDS

I believe that the number and proximity of close friends will differ from woman to woman. It will depend upon the intensity of our ministries; our styles of leadership; our personalities (extrovert vs. introvert); even perhaps our giftings (ie. mercy vs. prophetic); and the level of maturity in those in ministry around us.

We will find ourselves choosing our best friends and accountability partners carefully. Generally speaking, they will come from within the ranks of others in like-ministry circumstances. We will find that there is an immediate ease in connecting with them because we understand the dynamics of each other's ministry demands. There will, therefore, be less chance of offense when we simply haven't much free time. With women who are also in ministry we can move more quickly into intimacy—talking about deeper matters of the heart and spirit—not having to constantly first bridge the gap of differences in environment and calling.

It is easiest when these friends live nearby, but possible even at a distance. With email, communication can be almost daily, maintained through succinct messages that get to the heart of issues quickly. However, frequent visits with one another away from the ministry and the computer are critical. We need to look into one another's eyes and learn the expressions on each other's face. We need hugs and laughter and time to be girls together, leaving the "ministry" behind for a few hours. Refreshed, we will be able to return to our work with renewed vision and passion.

A DANGEROUS VOW

Vulnerability *will* bring the possibility of betrayal and pain. If we are betrayed, however, we must guard against making the vow to never let anyone close again. As painful as our wounds are, they *can* be healed through forgiveness and by identifying with Christ. We must never stop loving.

Isolationism—born out of self-protection—brings a detachment that stifles ministry, engenders false perceptions of others and limits our growth as caring human beings. Without authentically connecting with the people around us, ministry becomes a "me vs. them" thing; creates thrones; breeds loneliness; and thwarts accountability, making us more susceptible to bitterness and even moral failure in time.

We *must not* nurse wounds and cut ourselves off from those who offer us appropriate friendship. There *are* men and women whose friendships can minister to us deeply, even if for only a season. To these friends God will give the ability to help us stay in love with the unlovely around us. As they reflect God's heart to us, we will be nurtured and enriched time after time.

A CAUTION

Just as we must discern needy motives in others that could be dangerous to us if we try to be too intimate, we must discern when our own motives for friendships are wrong. We can be as guilty as anyone else of looking to human love to give us worth. It's at times like this that our accountability partner or mentor is indispensable to reflect back to us the truth and reconnect us with the love and approval of God. He alone can truly give us the validity and affirmation that endure, *never* betraying us.

LEVELS OF FRIENDSHIP

Friendship is not an all or nothing proposition. There are several levels on which friendship can be pursued. Most people look to us for a listening ear and gentle encouragement, not expecting us to be their buddies. Others will try to get close for selfish reasons, and with these we must set boundaries for which we shouldn't apologize. Friendship with them will be somewhat impersonal.

Many will offer us camaraderie in the faith, and with these, we can share ministry visions and dreams. A few will demonstrate the level of trustworthiness and maturity that will allow us to proceed to a more personal level of friendship. With these we will almost automatically "connect." They will not clutch at us, realizing that we are a gift to the Body. Their intent will be to encourage us and be a rear guard for us in prayer. They may or may not live nearby, but when we spend time together, we both are refreshed. Trust and intimacy will grow over time and through shared experiences. Such friendships will last a lifetime and will be a deep source of joy.

OUR FRIEND FOREVER

But, sometimes, even our dearest friends cannot be there for us. Sometimes they are in the midst of their own crises and have no emotional reserve for what we might be going through. Sometimes, as hard as we search for them, there are no hearts ready to share sustained pain with us, and no ears ready to hear our stories all the way to the end.

Even our spouses can become impatient or irritated when we try to explain to them a struggle in the ministry or in our emotions that has us ready to cry at the drop of a hat. It is not because they do not care, but because they feel helpless to solve it and just can't get a grip on how to comfort us as we need.

It's in those times that we remember: God is truly our most faithful, patient and understanding friend—a friend who will never let us down. His heart is always big enough for our pain and his understanding vast enough to know best how to comfort and encourage us. It's then that we finally run to Him, ashamed again that we too often wait until we have exhausted all other avenues of comfort before we do so.

And there He is, waiting for us. As we pour out our hearts to Him, He soothes our fears and mends us. Our sorrow gradually turns to hope and then to peace. We know that joy itself will come in the morning because we have cast ourselves into the loving arms of the very One Who loved us so much He went to hell and back to make us His friends.

There *will* be those times when no mortal is near to walk with us. That's when we remember to take the hand that was there all the time. Whether in good or bad times, however, let's learn to run to Him first!

ALL WILL BE WELL

God will guide us as we sort through the relationships in our lives. As we invite Him to search our hearts, He will give us the courage and wisdom to invest ourselves in others at each level—appropriately and wisely. As we grow in intimacy with Him, He will add those to our lives who will enrich us and for whom we can be a blessing in return. And through it all, He will be a friend that sticks closer than a brother or a sister. We will never be alone.

DISCUSSION PROBES:

1. Have you ever been betrayed by someone you trusted but who was angry with you?
   - How did you deal with your feelings?
   - Describe the process you pursued to find healing.
   - To what degree has the relationship been restored?
   - What did you learn through the experience?
2. Upon what scriptures would you lean in order to help you through the pain of broken friendships?
3. In what ways, if any, have you changed in your approach to friendships in the past few years?
   - What, if any, safeguards do you now have?
4. Describe ways to show respect for your friends and prevent your *own* unwitting neglect or wounding of them in the days ahead.
5. Are you inclined to have several close friends, or very few?
   - What are three outstanding characteristics of the person to whom you are the closest, besides your mate, if you are married?
6. What areas of your life do you most protect from those who are your casual friends?
7. How does your leadership style affect your friendships?
8. What part does loneliness play in your ministry role?
   - Where do you find comfort?
9. Explain the statement: *Isolationism—born out of self-protection—brings a detachment that stifles ministry, engenders false perceptions of others and limits our growth as caring human beings.*
10. To what degree does human love give you validation as a leader?
    - Has it replaced your validation by God?

Chapter Fifteen

GROWING THROUGH FAILURE

If the Lord delights in a man's way,
he makes his steps firm; though he stumble,
he will not fall, for the Lord upholds him with his hands.
Psalm 37:23, 24

Someone once said, "We are all failures—at least, all the best of us are." Making mistakes, letting others down, misjudging situations and committing any number of errors is part of being human. Denying our failures is foolhardy. Refusing to learn from them is a luxury we can't afford.

It is the most freeing experience to admit it when we are wrong and cease the charade that all is well. Perfectionism is a relentless taskmaster that has no mercy and provides no lasting success. Our natural minds tell us that we must hide our weaknesses—that no one will respect us if they know the truth. On the contrary, transparency and honesty—even about failure—will enhance our leadership, while pretense will breed distrust.

Growth comes through the embarrassing process of stumbling, identifying the cause of our imbalance, strengthening our muscles through repentance, taking wise counsel, adjusting the course and setting out again. Many times we will take 3 steps forward, fall back two, adjust and begin the climb again. This is progress.

Giving up is not an option when our vision is from God. Maturity and ministry effectiveness will be there when we arrive. If the process of growth is entered into, success is a given. What that success looks like is up to God and will be of a deeper nature than we had ever imagined when we first set out to serve Him.

MY OWN FAILURE

During the sixteen years that I was on staff at Teen Challenge Training Center, I thought I was a great teacher because of the praise I received. But God saw the insecurities and self-centeredness in my heart and not the "success." He knew that I desperately needed healing from past sorrow and to know who I was in Him, whether I was ever applauded again or not. He grieved over the struggles my husband and I had in trying to understand and love each other. Because God cared more about me and about my need for health, joy and freedom than about my "success" at Teen Challenge, He allowed me to fail.

In my quest for the "approval" I didn't feel at home, I became attached in heart and spirit to an intern who had been assigned to me to train. I knew nothing about boundaries and no one gave me any as the intern and I began working together. Because we were short of space, we shared a small office and developed a close friendship.

As we confided in each other about our hopes, dreams, sorrows and disappointments, the longing to give mutual comfort and happiness grew. We mistook our desire to rescue one another for love. By the time God revealed to me my deceptive, self-seeking heart, I was on the verge of destroying my family and ministry. (Read the full story in *Lambs on the Ledge*.)

I am convinced that the knitting of personal spirits and hearts that so easily occurs between sensitive, but emotionally unhealed—or discontent—ministry workers is *more* dangerous than sexual sin. If we sin sexually, it is blatantly obvious to all, and discipline comes swiftly. However, spiritual adultery can hide within our hearts for often great lengths of time, slowly but surely destroying our faithfulness to God and those closest to us. It becomes a matter of spiritual worship—worship at the altar of human love. We deem God's love as insufficient and grasp fulfillment from another as our inalienable right.

REPENTANCE AND DISCIPLINE

When I voluntarily confessed spiritual adultery to my supervisor at Teen Challenge and asked for help in separating from the intern, I was simply fired. Perhaps because I was the only woman on the teaching staff and the new Executive Director—with whom I had no history—was possibly distrustful of women in ministry, the penalty was unusually severe. But throughout the process, I knew that I was in the hands of God, not man, and that it was the *love of God* for my life that was bringing the breaking.

My repentance was deep and my cry real for a new heart that sought only God. During the fire of discipline, I hungered to be changed so that I wouldn't break the hearts of God and my family again. The discipline was profoundly sobering, but that's what it took to knock down everything false that propped up my self-life so that I could finally find my identity in God's true love.

REDEMPTIVE TRANSPARENCY

During the last two weeks of my employment, instead of hiding the reason I was leaving—as I had often seen dismissed staff do in the past—I taught all my classes on the roots and dangers of spiritual adultery. The Holy Spirit used my transparency to melt many hard hearts and bring forgiveness and repentance between several men and their wives. Perhaps more was accomplished spiritually during those two weeks of honesty about my failure than 16 years of "inspired" teaching.

As I experienced His forgiveness and comfort, I began to see my husband with God's eyes. How I grew during that experience! I wish we could have avoided hurting each other, but the pain drove us to the counseling we needed to remove the rotten roots in both of our lives. Our marriage has been refined by fire, and our commitment to one another is now, by grace, unshakable.

That failure did more to teach me of the unconditional love and power of God in my life than all the accolades I could have gained through ministry. Furthermore, only failure could have removed me from the comfort of teaching at Teen Challenge and launched the larger vision He has for my life. Failure brought correction to my course and ultimately healing for my marriage. I am still learning lessons from that time of failure.

AS WOMEN

For some of us, the greatest contributor to failure may be unresolved conflict stemming from our distrust or fear of male authority figures. As a result, we can't seem to speak with them truthfully or transparently. Whether that male is our husband or our boss in the ministry, the inability to communicate honestly becomes fertile ground for suspicion, defensiveness and gross misunderstanding. We find ourselves behaving childishly. When we do, we realize that this behavior is the same as that which we donned as daughters of fathers who didn't protect or nurture or listen to us—or whose approval we never could win.

In one way, I am very fortunate. My father *did* protect and nurture and listen to me. Therefore, I am more inclined to try to understand a male authority and communicate in a way that comes alongside him, rather than challenges or resists. I generally expect the best even when his attitude or communication is ambiguous. This ability is a treasured legacy from my dad.

Because my dad was so kind, my greatest longing was to please him and never embarrass him or make him sad. However, his *complete* approval always seemed just out of reach. As an adult, it therefore remained difficult for me to speak up when men around me behaved badly; I was hamstrung by my own fear of offending and my quest for approval.

Others of us may feel haunted by mothers who overshadowed us and stole our confidence, betrayed or abandoned us emotionally, or demanded more perfection than we could deliver. Within this dilemma, we only find healing by a revelation from God of how greatly He values us and how precious we are to Him. Our confidence and courage will come from the security we find in His patient, encouraging Spirit. There will be no hurdles to clear, no prizes to win to gain His approval, no arguing or complaining. As we release our mothers from our anger and resentment, our own personalities will be set free. Only then, will we be able to *believe* the affirmation others give us about our leadership potential.

Thank God, we can be freed from negative cycles through the power of Calvary, when we release our parents from our high and unfulfilled expectations of them and forgive them. As we cast the pain and judgments upon the Savior and let the cross break the control they unwittingly have had over us, God will give us a new way of seeing them. We will become suddenly aware that the malady that plagued us—the need for loving, affirming, protecting parents—likely plagued them as well when they were children! We need to let go of our impossible demands and turn to the heavenly Father, the only totally faithful and unselfish parent there ever has been.

We will find ourselves able to joyfully submit to our spiritual authorities and expect the best from their hands, which amazingly frees *them to give us their best*! We will be able to more clearly and objectively gauge right and wrong and be able to praise authentically, as well as appeal effectively for righteousness when he or she is off base.

ENDURING FAILURE

If our ministry has met with failure—or relationships within the ministry have been fractured—we will grieve deeply as we face the losses. Perhaps dreams have been destroyed; friendships have been altered forever; the future looks bleak and foreboding; and feelings of worthlessness will overcome us.

After I lost my job at Teen Challenge, I wept for months. Even though the leaders had honored me after my confession and repentance, there were no kind words under heaven that could soften the blow of not being able to return to my ministry there. The friendships I had cherished among staff were, for all practical purposes, over; my income had ended, and remorse engulfed me. Even though I blamed no one but myself, the loss of all that had been an integral part of my life for sixteen years left me feeling disconnected from meaning and dreadfully lonely.

Jim and I moved our family to Florida to begin again. We left our dream house that I had designed and decorated myself, and the kids left all their childhood friends and all that was familiar to them. It took Jim eight months to find work in Florida, and we slid into debt. The price we paid to start again was enormous, and the sorrow great.

Meanwhile, I wept and wept, even while the Holy Spirit was teaching me and mending my broken heart. There was *nothing* easy about it—*nothing*. But healing came, and we learned to love on a higher plane than ever before. Our foundations—laid afresh by God Himself as we were counseled to health—were solid at last, both in our marriage and our concepts of ministry. As we grieved and rebuilt, God redirected both our futures into *new* ministries—Jim's into Church Administration, and mine into writing and speaking on ministry and leadership issues. What the enemy had meant for evil, God had turned into good.

REBUILDING

For any of us after failure, grief needs to run its course once we have repented or forgiven. Just as when a loved one dies, mourning provides a healthy release. It's not wise to deny the losses and plunge into new ministry pursuits in an attempt to cover the pain. We will need time alone with God—probably many months of it—so that He can speak to us of His love for us again, and slowly restore us emotionally and spiritually. He will cradle us in His arms during the healing process. We will emerge stronger, wiser, more other-centered and less fearful. In His abiding presence, we will have discovered a new dignity and quiet humility that is slow to blame, quick to forgive.

And when rest has come and we no longer fear facing people—

or feel the need to justify or convince them of our innocence—a new vision will fill our hearts. Hope in God will have returned and the flame of our passion will be pure at last.

INEVITABLE

We *will* make mistakes. Those who minister with us will make mistakes. Any one of us is capable of the worst of sins. The lessons that come from these failures teach us about ourselves and give God the opportunity to do a transforming work in our lives—if we let the humbling come.

Personal failure can indicate:

1. Bitterness against past authority figures in our lives.
2. Hidden addictions from which we need deliverance.
3. Believing we are better than others and above the law.
4. Ungratefulness for God's dealings in our lives.
5. Deep regret over past choices.
6. Perfectionism, which breeds despair and anger at God.
7. Naivete about temptations and our vulnerability.

FAILURE OF PROJECTS

More often, our lessons come simply through the failure of *projects*. When projects fail, it is likely due to at least one of the following conditions:

1. The planning process wasn't sound.
2. The team hadn't been properly prepared.
3. The timing was wrong.
4. Conflicts among team members were not resolved promptly.
5. Lack of trust had developed because of unkept promises.

As we gain confidence from His love for us, we can go back over each of these issues, apologize for our errors, bring reconciliation, solicit input and advice, make alterations and pursue a freshly-tested plan.

FACING THE TRUTH

Failure is like a fuse that blows to warn us that something is amiss in our circuitry. It is a time to reassess and define causes. Change is always possible, and repentance cleans the slate, providing a fresh start. Discussions with all who had been involved about what went wrong and how the danger could be avoided next time brings great instruction to all.

The key ingredient is humility: facing ourselves honestly and confessing our sins—or the weaknesses of the plan—and asking forgiveness. Only God is perfect. We are in the process of being changed into His image...and we have a long way to go!

Amazingly, God chooses to perform His will on earth through us who fail so easily! Because He knows His own power to change lives, He doesn't fear our weaknesses but ceaselessly moves through events to give us opportunities to mature. If there are character flaws within the fabric of our lives, He will allow us to fail so that we too will see them and humbly ask for His divine correction.

God wastes not a single tear we shed over our failures—*if* we turn quickly and humbly to Him and our co-workers for forgiveness and correction. We will fail, and others will fail. Forgiveness, correction, cleansing and second chances should be a way of life among us in ministry. Pretending we are perfect, or refusing to deal compassionately with others' imperfections, breeds hypocrisy and brings no growth and no eternal success. Momentary success *impresses* people, but the way in which we face and learn from failure *impacts and changes* people.

SAVING GRACE

Mistakes and failures provide precious opportunities to lean more deeply into the heart of God. As we learn from Him, our vision grows clearer on the journey. Wisdom is gained as we travel; the rocks over which we stumbled in the early days are detected quickly and avoided. But best of all, we know beyond a shadow of a doubt that God is with us and is on our side to bring ultimate victory—that the world know Him and His saving grace.

DISCUSSION PROBES:

1. How do you feel when you hear the word "failure?"
   - Are you determined never to fail?
2. Describe a situation where you or someone you know was drawn emotionally/spiritually to a co-worker.
   - What was the result?
   - How can such a dangerous knitting of hearts be avoided? (See Chapter 11 in my book, *Instruments for His Glory.*)
3. How do you personally deal with any neglect or lack of affirmation by the primary men in your life?
4. What part can God's love play in preventing sexual sin?
   - To what degree is His love enough for you?
5. Share a failure story from your life.
   - Have you recovered completely?
   - What lessons did you learn through it?
6. Describe the grieving and rebuilding processes following failure.
7. What is different in your heart and life that would prevent a repeat of that failure?
8. Study the list of indications of failure on p. .
   - Do you sense traces of any of these in your life?
   - Share it with someone who can counsel you and pray for you.

9. Develop a plan to examine project failure to be used the next time a project hits the skids.
10. Examine the seasons of your life and ministry.
    - What part has failure played in your growth and in redirecting you for a greater purpose than before you failed?

Section Four:

EMBRACING THE JOURNEY

Chapter Sixteen

CONFIDENCE
IN CHRIST

Such confidence as this is ours through Christ before God. Not that we are competent in ourselves to claim anything for ourselves, but our competence comes from God. He has made us competent as ministers of a new covenant—not of the letter but of the Spirit...
2 Corinthians 3:4-5

The fruit of our growth as leaders is formed in the quiet dignity that comes from knowing we are valued by God and created for a purpose. Such confidence protects us from the ravages of people pleasing and the energy-draining gymnastics of having to prove ourselves over and over to people bent on bolstering their *own* importance. His perfect love lodged deep in our hearts casts out fear and defuses anger. No matter what we face, His presence will carry us home.

We will desperately need this kind of confidence when we must deny someone's passionate plea for an action that we know is out of sync with God's plan for the day. Such confidence will bring healing more quickly—and forgiveness more easily—when we are judged and defamed for doing instead what we know will ultimately bring more growth in those around us.

IN THE FACE OF OBJECTIONS

Several years ago, I was in a season during which God was using me significantly in counseling women who had been abused or who had controlling behavior patterns. I tried to do everything right. I was careful to maintain boundaries around my life, not letting them call at all hours and limiting our sessions to a specific length of time. I told them that I loved them in Christ, but that I was not their savior. My purpose was to compassionately take them to Jesus for healing. Everything I taught was to shift their dependence from people to God.

After counseling one particularly controlling lady through many painful memories and seeing great improvement, I sensed clearly that God wanted me to draw the sessions to an end. It was time for her to walk on her own in the freedom that had overtaken her. I knew that she had a firm grasp on how to remain free and respond wisely to the unchanged conditions in her extended family that were beyond her control.

But rather than being grateful for my help and excited about entering into a new realm of confidence in Christ, she turned on me with a vengeance.

"You call yourself a Christian? You're supposed to love others, not shut them out when they need you! You're nothing but a hypocrite!" she screamed at me.

Her response shot through me like a knife. I had gone through a lot in counseling her and had given her all that I could. Up until then, she had seemed very appreciative. Her sudden turning on me was a shock.

This can easily happen in ministry, especially with women who want to control us or become knit to us in dependency. If we don't have the confidence to take unpopular stands, we will be dogged endlessly by others' expectations and demands.

In this case, especially since her biggest problem had been manipulating, I couldn't let her intimidate me. For her own good, I stood firm. However, I wrote her a letter reaffirming all the changes that God had made in her life and challenged her to test His faithfulness. I said nothing about the way she had treated me, leaving conviction up to the Holy Spirit.

A few years later, after we had moved to Virginia, she surprised me by calling to tell me about all the victories she had been having in her life. She was free! She had found God faithful and she wanted me to know. How I rejoiced with her!

STANDING ALONE

In other matters as well, we will have to stand alone in what God is saying to us. We will, for instance, see the vision He has for our people before anyone else around us does. Our worth to the ministry will not be proven by accommodating others' doubts or compromising what God has called us to do. It will rather be proven by a consistency in hearing from God and acting courageously upon our convictions—while remaining respectful of others and honoring God's timing.

When God was stirring my heart to raise up women in leadership, I kept it to myself until I was certain of the procedure God wanted me to follow. I don't think that the men and women around me at the time would have believed that the vision was from God. The vision came five years before the evangelical church and the publishing industry would be ready for it. Because I never liked to make waves—people pleaser that I had always been—I tried to jump ship on the issue many times. If I had given up, *Instruments for His Glory* would not have been written, nor would I then have attempted this book. But again, God would not let me go. I have had to learn to stand *graciously* and *humbly* against the tides of either opposition or apathy in order to fulfill His purposes for my life.

FOREVER CONNECTED

Sometimes, because our visions can be unsettling to others—or because we foolishly and mistakenly imagine that the world has come to rest upon *our* shoulders—we begin to think we are "unique." We then concoct our own code of behavior—omitting common courtesy and vulnerability, relegating them to the domain of the ordinary and average. Aloofness and isolation soon follow.

Yes, we are special to God and one-of-a-kind, but so is everyone else! We are not a separate breed entitled to behave with insensitivity or to withdraw from intimacy with others in the Body. Vulnerability to others keeps us authentic, in touch with our humanness and aware of our need for God. Closeness with others also gives us the opportunity for valuable feedback and input as well as good old-fashioned fun.

"Uniqueness" and the isolation that it fosters, on the other hand, invariably breed a god mentality during success, and a martyr complex during hard times. Either way, our source of confidence shifts from Christ to our own prowess and supposed-superiority. This is an abomination to God.

It is only as we cast the vision *within* the context of Body life that we stay attuned to God's concerns and God's strategies for the challenges that are all around us. It's through working in tandem with those around us, in pursuit of the vision, that He will do His mighty works. We are one of many—indeed, one of a vast multitude who yearn to do the Father's will and leave this world a better place for our having been here.

LIKE CHILDREN

Constantly, we must return to what God values: the fruit of the spirit—love, joy, peace, patience, kindness, goodness, faithfulness, gentleness and self-control (Gal. 5:22-23)—that only come from intimacy with Him and a willingness to grow in our relationships with others. Then, as we daily invite the Holy Spirit to fill us, instruct us in the wisdom of God and give us the ability to obey, His power will be manifest. It's His life moving within us, most easily embraced when we shed the trappings of human "greatness," that works miracles and causes us to lead with true authority.

HOPE THAT DOESN'T DISAPPOINT

1 Thess. 5:16 says to be joyful always; pray continually; give thanks in all circumstances, for this is God's will for us in Christ Jesus. Leadership is no easy task. Romans 5:3-5 says that we also rejoice in our sufferings, because we know that suffering produces perseverance; perseverance, character; and character, hope. And this hope does not disappoint us, because God has poured out His love into our hearts by the Holy Spirit, whom he has given us.

His love is the bedrock, the anchor for everything. It is the one thing on which our hope and confidence are grounded and secured. Because He loves us, we know that there will be a great story to tell when we have learned to serve with passion and grace. He is not a God who intends to make our hearts sick, so He will not defer hope beyond our endurance. And, meantime, we will be changed somehow.

Childlike faith in His character—which knows nothing of despair, and everything about hope and God's irresistible love—will give us the confidence to see visions through to reality. In this confidence, we will stand.

So do not throw away your confidence;
it will be richly rewarded. You need to persevere
so that when you have done the will of God,
you will receive what he has promised.
Heb. 10:35-36.

DISCUSSION PROBES:

1. Think back to a time when someone tried to attach himself/herself to you to satisfy his/her own need for acceptance and value.
   - What was the context?
   - What were the symptoms of this unhealthy attachment?
2. How have you handled extricating yourself from needy, but never growing, individuals?
   - How did they react?
   - What was the outcome?
   - What did you learn?
3. Because people have a tendency to elevate leaders—sometimes bordering on worship—have you ever slipped into believing your own press and thinking you were above others?
   - Within this context, how did you relate to others, especially those with the gifts of helps or giving?
   - Did you assume that they were there to expressly serve you?
4. Is there anything in your life or ministry such as voice, appearance, youth, intelligence, physical stamina, spouse or a certain friendship that, if you lost it, you'd feel as though you had lost your value to God?
5. What are your greatest fears in life and ministry?
6. What has God said in His Word that could give you hope and confidence in the event of great loss?
7. Twila Paris wrote a moving worship song entitled, *What Am I Without You?* In it she says, "What am I but a piece of earth—breathing holy breath?" How can that truth give you hope and worth in Christ?
8. Has God given you a vision for the Body of Christ that others find hard to understand?
   - How can you tell whether to keep silent and wait or to speak it forth to inspire or challenge others?
   - If you are ridiculed or opposed, how will you respond redemptively?
9. Describe a situation in which you were persecuted as a leader

and retaliated by defensiveness, criticism, withdrawal or bitterness.
- How would you handle it differently today?

10. Have you ever experienced "hope deferred" that made your heart sick? In what or whom was your hope?
    - What does Heb. 11:13 say about godly hope?
    - Are you willing to press on even with the possibility that your vision won't be fulfilled in your lifetime?

Chapter Seventeen

COMMUNING
WITH GOD

As the deer pants for streams of water,
so my soul pants for you, O God.
Psalm 42:1

*Deep calls to deep in the roar of your waterfalls...*vs. 7a

The journey through ministry leadership is both arduous and exhilarating, and the only way we will keep on course and reach our destination emotionally healthy and spiritually sane is by pursuing the presence of God. When we commune with Him as a lifestyle—escaping the crowds regularly to simply rest in His arms and draw strength from His presence—the pull of our flesh to compromise, our fear of failure and the temptation to be great in others' eyes lose their power.

Alone with Him, a precious simplification takes place. We are children again. Ministry and all its demands are returned to Him to lift and weigh. Through the calm that descends as we spend intimate time alone with Him—walking in the woods, sitting beside a quiet stream or standing by the sea gazing out across the waves to the horizon—life is cleared of its debris.

He loves us and wants us ever near. He's waiting for us everyday! God has been watching us through the years—hearing and answering our cries—and now he's waiting for us to spend time with Him in solitude. He waits for us to let all other pursuits fall away to just *be* with Him. He waits for each of us to understand the joy He takes in us.

We forget that He already knows *us* intimately, as David describes in Ps. 139:13-16.

And now He wants us to know *Him* intimately as well.

Remember when Jesus wept over Jerusalem? He longed to draw His people into His embrace, but they wouldn't come! When we long, in return, for intimacy with Him, we are merely echoing *His* desire and cry! But he expects much more than lip service; in fact, in John 17, Jesus prayed that our relationship with Him would be as intimate as His was with the Father. Amazing!

For this we were created: *To know Him and commune with Him*—to embrace and love Him Who first loved us. David writes in Ps. 139:17-18 that God's thoughts are centered on us constantly! Zeph. 3:17 says that He sings over us! He dreams for us, He plans for us and He moves mountains for us.

And He waits for us to love Him with abandonment and passion.

Pursuing intimacy with Him goes beyond our regular times in the Word or travailing in prayer for others. It's about leaving it all in preference to His precious company. It's about being refilled by His Spirit and hearing from His heart what we never could have predicted while steeped in the "rational" pursuits of ministry. It requires intentional time alone with Him, without an agenda.

He meets us in solitude—especially in natural settings, away from the evidence of the works of man. Alone with Him, His perspective becomes ours, and our wills come into line with His. Alone with Him, we learn to sense His moods and hear His voice. (If we don't learn to hear His voice in solitude, how will we ever distinguish it within the noise and busyness of ministry?)

HIS CALL TO US

Even as a child on my father's farm, I knew He was calling me away with Him. And I followed—often for long walks in the woods that covered the hillside limits of our property, and then back along the creek that threaded its way through the ravines on its way down to the valley. All through my youth, I knew His presence and dreamed of His majesty. I loved being His little girl. I remember making up songs of praise and love for Him long before "contemporary music" was born. To this day, communing with Him is my greatest joy.

And this longing to be alone with Him out in nature pursues me daily. If I miss a few days due to inclement weather, I feel as though I might suffocate or die from a broken heart! I know that sounds melodramatic, but my own need to be utterly embraced by Him in a solitary place is intense.

Many times during these recent years of writing, frustrated by some impasse in the writing process, I have called my husband on the phone at work for encouragement. After listening for a few moments, he'd usually ask gently, "Have you been to your swing in the woods yet today?" at which I'd hang up in relief and run for the woods to be with Him.

On the way there, I'd figuratively drop my cares in the bushes beside the path. My purpose in going to Him was not to get Him to solve my problems but just to *be* with Him. On the swing with Him, life would become simple again—and I'd remember that my love was all He had ever asked of me. *That* I could give, even if I never wrote or spoke another word of significance to the human race.

I must admit, however, that even though I took no list of needs to Him at those times, He sometimes addressed them anyway. On those occasions, just as I hopped from the swing and headed home refreshed, He'd drop a wonderfully creative idea into my mind that would solve the impasse in my writing that had driven me there.

It was always a gift, pure and simple. Many times through the years the gifts have arrived after spending intentional time in His presence—unsought answers, ideas and perceptions. But I don't *seek* them during these reprieves; I seek His sweet presence alone. I am no longer surprised, however, that absorbing His presence yields enlightenment from Him. His presence brings light itself to every dark corner and unravels every mystery. He's at work all the time in our lives...and sometimes He tells us about it.

STAYING STRONG

We cannot possess or maintain the passion for ministry that will martial forces, win mighty spiritual battles and hold us steady during defeat without continuous intimacy with God. Passion for Him is the fire of fires.

If we don't nurture and find freedom in expressing our passion for God, we will soon switch to ministering out of our human passion for purpose. This human passion can be perverted by ambition or snuffed out by deep disappointments or persecution. We are not called to die for missions but to give our lives to Him in love.

I fear that this may sound too ethereal. But I must take that risk because the challenge to pursue the mystery of God and the elusive, unpredictable wonder of His life within and without us must be met—no matter how it can or cannot be rationally described. In Western culture, we have become so self-sufficient and affluent, we can run great ministries for amazingly long periods of time without intimacy with God and the power of the Holy Spirit. But the inevitable crash into disillusionment when it all falls apart warns us to beware. All other leadership instruction is worthless without this point on the utter necessity of intimacy with the Father being made. Jesus withdrew from the crowds and the urgency of their distress in preference to solitude with His Father. The greater the demands on His life and ministry, the more quickly He retreated alone. It was in those hours that His strength for the call was restored and made sure. Dare we do less?

REFLECTION

The discipline of writing has helped develop the more reflective side of my nature. It has forced me to be quiet—to listen from *within,* instead of from without to all the voices around me. God speaks quietly to me, deep within, by His Spirit Who lives there. While, at times, I have railed against the arduous task of crafting words and ideas on paper, preferring to teach—and perhaps occasionally relying on visible enthusiasm and personal persuasion—I am certain that this discipline has stretched my spiritual senses.

I imagine that is why most spiritually influential leaders journal. So much is made clear during reflection! But a step beyond written reflection is the reflection that takes place alone with God in our solitary places. Because we don't write during these times, we must embrace fully the moment for the preciousness of His nearness, not for even the lessons we are learning. We who teach might be tempted to turn every insight into instruction for others; however, solitude most often delivers an insight meant for us alone.

Something amazing happens when we realize that He will speak to us for no other reason than that He loves being with us! When we realize that His interest in us is not in how we can take His words and make them be of benefit to others, we fairly explode with significance! What healing for low self esteem!

INTIMACY WITH GOD

No one taught us any more about intimacy with God than did David. It is no surprise that the man who valued God's presence above all the riches and power earth could offer had met God first alone out in the countryside as a shepherd. There his heart was won and shaped by the King of Kings.

Love for us as well is born in solitude; our hearts learn His melodies in solitude; character and the certainty of eternity take root in solitude. The values and strengths of every leader—and every disciple—are established while alone with God, and not by religious arguments which can fall when the winds of change blow. No amount of Bible study alone, no debate or mighty sermons replace the voice of the Holy Spirit in cementing our spiritual lives and purposes.

It may be difficult for some of us to find natural solitude because of the congestion of cities and the pressured pace of our culture. But it must be done. When I move to a new city, the very first thing I scout

out is the park system in that area. I have always been able to find a place in nature where I can be alone with God, even if I live in an apartment complex as I do now. If we are intentional about it, God will lead us to our special place to be alone with Him in His creation.

RETREATS

I cannot leave this subject without encouraging one more aspect of solitude: Retreats—extended times away with God. At least once a year each of us needs to go away by ourselves—or at the most with our spouse or best friend—to simply wait on God.

Away with Him in a quiet place for several days, we will experience a cleansing as the Holy Spirit convicts of sins and slights, and we repent and forgive. He not only clarifies His present purposes for our lives, but helps us cast vision for the future. Our pursuits will be either confirmed or changed as we seek His mind in the matter, free of the tyranny of the urgent and others' well-meaning voices. At these times, we should journal in order to ensure our commitments to resolves, decisions and convictions.

Twice a year, my husband and I go to Bradenton, Florida, on the Gulf side of the state, to be refreshed, cleansed and redirected. We arrive on the beach early when we know we will have it to ourselves. We pray, read, meditate and reflect to each other our passions in ministry and where we sense God is taking us. On paper we revisit our personal visions and mission statements, make adjustments and then sort out with each other how God is directing us to proceed.

No place seems to work better for us than the white Gulf beaches where the azure waves lazily lap the shore, soothing our nerves, quieting our hearts and reminding us of the constancy and gentle motion of God's power in our lives. We feel very finite in contrast to the vast Gulf waters, which puts our struggles into perspective and causes us to worship our great Creator with renewed admiration and devotion.

Whether it's at a cabin in the woods, by a remote lake, in the desert or on the beach, an intentional retreat is invaluable at setting us right again and restoring our physical strength, emotional peace and spiritual fire. If we think we are indispensable to our ministries and cannot leave for this time of assessment and reflection, we have not led well. Others *need* us to go away so that they can be trusted and rise to the occasion of managing well while we are gone. For their sakes as well as ours, we must take the time.

We never want to end up spiritually hollow, dusty and dry—chugging wearily along on yesterday's memories of intimacy! Solitude, reflection and retreat supply the lifeblood for our ministries and provide milestones in our love affair with God. Nothing else we do will replace these or be as important. Within these, we meet and hear from God—loved to life over and over again.

DISCUSSION PROBES:

1. Where do you go for solitude?
   - Do you go with an agenda, or only to commune with God?
   - To what extent do you believe that God longs for your company?
2. Describe a time of when God spoke to you while in solitude.
   - What did you learn from that experience?
3. How can your time in solitude affect your decisions in ministry?
   - Describe either an example of when communing with God saved you from making a serious mistake in judgment, or an example of when you wished you had sought Him but didn't and made a bad decision as a result.
4. How much time do you spend per week in solitude and reflection, compared to the time spent in ministry activity?
   - Is that amount of time adequate?
5. What did Jesus retreat into solitude at the height of the crowd's neediness?
   - How will you apply His example to your life?
6. Do you feel guilty for retreating without a project in hand? Why?
   - Are these concerns valid?
7. Do you take the time to reflect by journaling?
   - How can this help?
8. Where and in what environment do you feel closest to God?
   - Have you sensed the healing that a natural setting can induce?
9. Interview someone you consider an outstanding spiritual leader.
   - What roles do solitude, reflection and retreat play in his/her life?
10. If you do not currently employ solitude, reflection and retreat within your ministry schedule, are you willing to discipline yourself to do so?
    - What is your plan and when will you begin?

CONCLUSION

BEING FOUND FAITHFUL

Let us hold unswervingly to the hope we profess,
for he who promised is faithful.
Hebrews 10:23

Our personal goals have a way of defining who we are at any given moment. In the beginning of our journey into ministry leadership, our eyes are fixed on grand goals of great exploits in the name of God. But as time wears on—if we have been listening and learning anything at all—our gaze turns upward and outward.

My own personal goals have changed over the years, sifted through the fingers of God and refined within the fires of conviction, molded anew by His *true love* that will not let me go. After 25 years in ministry, these personal goals have become resolutely established at the core of my life:

1. To know Him intimately and to worship Him with my very life.
2. To know myself by His Spirit.
3. To see others with His eyes and value them as He does.
4. To be constantly learning from all I see and experience.
5. To remain a child, but to teach with His wisdom, enabling others to go further than I have gone.
6. *To be found faithful.*

TO BE FOUND FAITHFUL

That last goal repeatedly stirs up great emotion within me. Tears fill my eyes when I reflect on what it means to be faithful—faithful to Jesus Who has given me His very life, through the Holy Spirit, to enable me to finish this journey with passion and grace.

THE POWER OF THE HOLY SPIRIT

Amazingly, Jesus promised to never leave us nor forsake us. He even said we would do all that He had done and more, because He was going to the Father and would send the Holy Spirit to lead us into all truth. We will never be faithful to the end without the power and presence of the Holy Spirit within us. Furthermore, we will not have a clue how to lead redemptively—coalescing sometimes-renegade individualists into powerful teams that will move mountains on their knees—without His counsel. *Without* the Holy Spirit's power working in our lives, convicting, encouraging and teaching us the heart and ways of the Savior, we might as well throw in the towel right now. We cannot lead "so great a people" without Him. We may try to go it alone, but if we do, we will most assuredly live to regret it—not because God will be cruel to us, but because we will find ourselves frighteningly hollow and with nothing to show for our labor at the end of the journey.

CHANGED INTO HIS LIKENESS

As we are learning the deep lessons within surrender to His

lordship in all things, God is burning His initials into the palms of our hands and causing His image to be seen through the windows of our souls. We become different.

Slowly but surely, we grow wise to the sinister voice of the Accuser of the Brethren—that old serpent who never tires of trying to dishearten us with his lies—and we fall in love with obedience. Less and less often must we make the inevitable sacrifice that comes with rebellion.

We can at last tell the difference between having our own way, and seeing beyond our arguments to His greater purpose. In fact, we have discovered that the very worst and most lonely place is that in which we wander when we are unteachable know-it-alls. And we now sigh wearily when we find those individuals within our spheres of authority who are just that. We know that we must brace ourselves for a long, tedious duel with defiance, and be prepared to bear their attempts at revenge and justification that will eat up precious hours, days and years of valuable service.

THE MUSIC WITHIN SURRENDER

What enables us to endure the postponements and the flailing flesh of the immature, and simply cling to the vision that has burned in our hearts for what seems like centuries? Have we not decided to give faithfulness in return for faithfulness? Instead of acting out the faithfulness we once defined as God's constant upholding of all *our efforts*, our faithfulness has come to rest upon nothing but His character and the love songs He sings to us in the darkest hours of our deepest nights.

But I promise we will never hear those songs if we will not let everything be subject to His will, whether that will is clear or not! It is only as we count ourselves His willing slaves, remaining teachable to the core and spiritually hungry to the bone, that we will be able to identify His voice.

SUCCESS IN GOD'S KINGDOM

Through the paradoxes in Matthew 5, Jesus prophetically

described those who would be faithful to Him to the end, then and now. *Blessed are the poor in spirit*—those know their own depravity and utter dependence upon God. *Blessed are those who mourn*—those who grieve over the losses that sin brings and feel the pain of others. *Blessed are the meek*—those whose power to react in self-centeredness is under the control of the Holy Spirit.

Blessed are those who hunger and thirst for righteousness—those who long to be like Him and who will pay the price to pursue His character. *Blessed are the merciful*—those who extend to others what they themselves have so desperately needed and received during their own epic failures. *Blessed are the pure in heart*—those who are washed clean of selfish ambition.

Blessed are the peacemakers—those who yield their own rights to ease another into an understanding of the higher call of love. *Blessed are those who are persecuted because of righteousness*—those who have so identified with Christ that they are hated because they are like Him. *Blessed are you when people insult you, persecute you and falsely say all kinds of evil against you because of Me*—those who have chosen to align themselves with the faithful who never give up.

From within this faithfulness, we will be willing to lose our lives to find them, and die to live, counting it all joy. Any other kind of leadership is simply clever technique and sensible psychology, which even atheists can master. By daily living within an exchange of faithfulness with our heavenly Father, we will see hearts changed and mountains moved.

PREPARE TO FINISH

We are all truly runners in a great race. When we begin amidst the cheers of the people, euphoria surrounds us. Adrenaline pounds through our bodies as dreams of breaking the ribbon at the finish line fill our vision. It's as though the success—in having effectively set the pace that has energized a myriad of other runners who have trained at our sides—is within arm's reach.

For the first leg of the race, the sun is shining down upon us. A refreshing breeze is blowing and the cheers of our fans can still be heard in the distance. Feeling fit and trim, having studied hard and become equipped and trained by the best, we move rhythmically down the track. Not far behind us are those who have seasoned their own performance by learning from us.

But then the weather turns foul; a storm moves in and the heavy rains fall. As the fog silences the voices of those behind us, the loneliness seems overwhelming.

And the finish line now seems a million miles away. The hills sap our strength, the valleys are desolate and devoid of any sound but the slapping of our weary feet upon the sodden soil. Thoughts that we may not have been ready for such a test—that someone else should have been chosen to run—nag us hourly.

We begin to doubt our motives. Maybe we were just in it for ourselves after all. Maybe we were simply misguided glory seekers and not fit to participate. And as our aching muscles scream for a rest, we wonder why we ever cared.

But just as we are about to fall to the edge of the path, an unsolicited cry rises from the depths of our souls to the One Who called us to race in the very beginning. *Jesus, give me strength. Be my strength! Don't let me lose the prize I have given my life to win!*

And then, as He clears the fog away, we see it through the waning light—the finish line.

At that moment, all the discipline, training and prayer we faithfully embraced in the past reestablishes our pace. It's as though the Holy Spirit puts wings on our feet and drives our legs like relentless pistons toward the goal. We will finish, and we will finish well! By His grace, we will be found faithful.

THE ULTIMATE CALL

No matter what our influence in the Kingdom of God may be, faithfulness to the One Who keeps His word is the ultimate call. Being true to Him will prove more valuable than all the worthy plans we formulate or the visions we cast. He Who is faithful and true—Who planted the dreams in our hearts so long ago—will bring them to pass if we will trust Him fully.

Leadership begins and ends with faithfulness to the God Who

loves us. Within the sense and security of our relationship with Him, we will be able to hear His voice in critical times when reason fails. Furthermore, we will have the grace to forgive betrayal and continue to serve unselfishly. We will also be at peace even if no one ever recognizes the vastness of our influence whether behind the scenes or out in the limelight. And we will know how to wait without losing hope. And if He asks us to step down at the height of our influence, we will do so without a backward glance.

He must be all we need. Out of that fullness, regardless of how many or few future leaders we have developed or how great or small our influence, we will be *leading with passion and grace.*

And when we see Him in heaven one day, the words we long to hear will fill our hearts with victory: *Well done, good and faithful servant, well done.*

APPENDIX

A LEADER'S
PATH TO FREEDOM

I must:

1. Honor my parents: Forgive and release them. Ex. 20:12; Pr. 20:20, 30:17; Luke 6:37-38; I John 1:9.

2. Repent of believing lies about myself: Seek God's view. Ps. 139:1-18; John 15:9, 12-13; Luke 12:32; I Peter 3:9.

3. Break the curse of the past by repenting of bitter root judgments and expectations. Release judgment to God. Matt. 7:1-2; Gal. 6:7-8; Luke 6:37-38; Matt. 16:19, 18:18-20.

4. Confess and repent of my own sins (sexual, idolatry, selfishness, addictions, ignorance). Accept God's forgiveness. I Jn. 1:9; Matt. 6:12; Luke 13:3; Acts 17:30; Rom. 6:11-14; Isa. 30:15, 18; Isa. 44:23.

5. Ask God to cleanse my body, soul and spirit from past defilement. Ps. 51; Heb. 9:14, 10:22; Mark 1:41.

6. Know and believe what God says in His Word. Ps. 34:17-18; Rom. 4:3, 20-25; Rom. 5:9-11, 17, 10:9-13.

7. Learn to listen to the Holy Spirit and be held accountable for my behavior. Heb. 12:14-15; Ps. 37:3-6, 42:8; John 16:5-15; Rom. 8:27; Pr. 19:20.

8. Avoid compromising situations and people. Guard my heart. Rom. 12; Rom. 8; Eph. 6:10-18; Mal. 3:13-16; Pr. 4:23.

9. Rejoice and be grateful that His glory has been restored to my life!

TAKE THESE BONDAGES AND BREAK THEM. I DON'T WANT THEM ANYMORE:

-
-
-

PRAYER FOR HEALING

I surrender my self-centeredness, my sins and my wounds to you, Lord. I forgive those who have sinned against me, and I cease seeking revenge through anger or withholding love. I repent of the bitter root judgments I have made against others and ask you to break the power those judgments have had to control my behavior. I want to be completely free to discover who I am in you!

Lord, fill me with your life and your presence in a fresh and powerful way. Draw me to your side daily. Be lord of every secret area of my life. No longer will I hide from you and others.

Father, teach me how to honor you and others with great love and faithfulness. May I be a blessing to all who know me. Make me like you!

Thank you for the miracle of a heart that has been set free! Show me how to live by *A Higher Call*—the call to carry your life with genuine love, transparency and joy.

SCRIPTURAL CHARACTERISTICS OF AN EFFECTIVE LEADER

Scriptures from NIV

1. Understands and owns the vision and mission and can communicate it in a way that others understand (Neh. 2:5, 11-18; Joshua 1:10)
2. Filled with a passion—rooted in unselfish love—to take others on to higher ground in fulfilling the vision (Neh. 1:3-4; John 3:16-17; John 15:16a; John 17:20-23; Col. 2:2-3)
3. Inspires others and moves them to action (Joshua 1:17-18; Mk. 16:15-18; 2 Cor. 9:2b; Lk. 10:1-11)
4. Teachable; knows he or she isn't the final authority on anything; seeks others' insights (Ps. 25:4-5; Pr. 12:15)
5. Flexible; willing to make hard choices in order to more effectively equip and empower others (Pr. 27:23;1 Jn. 3:16; Mt. 26:42)
6. An encourager (Col. 1:3-6; Col. 3:15-17; Acts 15:32; Heb. 3:13)

7. Vulnerable; transparent; truthful; honest; trustworthy (Pr. 10:9; Pr. 11:3; Pr. 24:26; Pr. 28:13)

8. Desires to be held accountable; not a lone ranger (1 Pet. 2:13; Pr. 27:12)

9. Able and willing to say "I was wrong. Please forgive me." (Ps. 32:5; Pr. 28:13)

10. A sensitive listener; gives undivided attention (Pr. 4:20; Pr. 25:20; Phil. 2:1-4)

11. Knows that the ministry belongs to God, not to him or her (Col. 1:25)

12. Receives counsel regularly from someone wise and trusted (Pr. 12:18; Pr. 16:20)

13. Keeps areas of his or her life in balance (Pr. 31:26-28)

14. Knows how to handle praise without succumbing to pride (Pr. 3:34; Pr. 27:2; Gal. 5:26)

15. Is being mentored by someone more highly skilled in leadership (Jn. 6:3; Jn. 13:12-17; 1 Tim. 1:18)

16. Is deeply committed to a local body of believers (Acts 14:26-27;Heb. 10:23-25)

17. Loves seeing others succeed beyond his or her own level of success (Col. 1:28; 1 Cor. 10:24)

18. Knows how to correct in love and is committed to restoring that person (Gal. 6:1-3)

19. Knows how to handle conflict; not afraid to confront (Eph. 5:11)

20. Not controlled by approval; able to take an unpopular stand when he or she knows it is right (Pr. 29:25; Gal. 2:11)

21. Doesn't judge; understands that he or she doesn't know the whole story and that final judgment is God's job, not his or hers (Mt. 7:1-2; Jn. 5:27; Jer. 17:9; Ro. 2:16)

22. Models the behavior he or she expects from others (1 Cor. 4:16; 1 Thes. 1:6)

23. Desires to work with others of complementary gifting, knowing the result will be more effective than doing it all himself or herself; seeks unity (Ps. 133; Eph. 4:3; Eph. 4:11-13, 16)

24. Has resolved past injuries; is not bitter; has a heart that quickly forgives (Eph. 4:32; Gal. 6:7-8; Mt. 6:14; Mk. 11:25)

25. Willing to relinquish position and rest when counseled to do so; trusts God with his or her life and ministry; embraces discipline when needed (Pr. 2:11; Pr. 3:11-12; Pr. 10:17; Pr. 12:1; Pr. 15:22; Pr. 19:21; Pr. 27:9)
26. Is loyal; never disrespects others (1 Jn. 3:16-18; Pr. 20:20)
27. Exhibits courage and tenacity (Eph. 6:10-18; 2 Tim. 1:7)
28. Is sensitive to God's timing (Ps. 27:13-14; Ps. 3:14-15; Pr. 16:3)
29. Shares information freely; not territorial (Phil. 2:3; Pr. 11:25; Gal. 6:6, 10)
30. Exhibits common sense (Pr. 25:11; 2 Tim. 1:7)
31. Respects others' individuality (1 Pet. 2:17a; Eph. 5:21; Phil. 2:3-4)
32. Deeply values those who follow; understands stewardship of their lives; protects and defends (Phil. 4:3; Ps. 16:3; Eph. 4:1-4, 15-16)
33. Self-disciplined and in control of his or her emotions and words (Pr. 17:27; Pr. 14:29; Gal. 5:22-23)
34. Approachable and generous (Jesus' example: Mt. 11:28; Mt. 14:14; Mt. 19:14; Mt. 10:42; and 2 Cor. 9:6; 1 Jn. 3:17)
35. Honors commitments and keeps his or her word (Num. 30:2; Mt. 5:37; Pr. 16:3; Pr. 25:14)
36. Prays daily for those whom he or she leads (Phil. 1:3-6; Col.1:9-12)
37. Has a committed circle of people who pray daily for him or her (Eph. 6:19-20)
38. Has a sense of humor (Pr. 17:22)
39. Delights in people, but never fosters a personal following (Phil. 1:6; Pr. 22:4; Pr. 27:21)

NOTE: No matter how gifted or spiritual we may be, if we do not have a passion for the vision and mission of the ministry we are in, we are not a good choice for a leader within that ministry. Everyone must be headed in the same direction. Leadership is not about serving ourselves and our projects or talents. Leaders must desire to be knit with one another, adjusting and cooperating to reach a clear, common and measurable goal.

OUR BIBLICAL MENTORS IN LEADERSHIP

1. **Moses:** Cast the vision; assembled the team; pressed on when there was no end in sight; paid the price so that the next generation could be free

2. **Joshua:** Multiplied the vision; acted fearlessly; believed God for direction in every battle

3. **Deborah:** Judged wisely; inspired others; led courageously in battle; didn't seek her own glory; brought the people back to God

4. **Esther:** Waited for God's timing; honored authority; risked her life to rescue others and right a wrong

5. **Nehemiah:** Assessed, planned and delegated; used diplomacy; restored holiness

6. **Joseph:** Was faithful in obscurity; built trust by his own respect for others; resisted bitterness and continued to love those who had wronged him; would not dishonor his leader

7. **David:** Was transparent; built for the future; valued his relationship with God above all else; repented willingly; embraced discipline thoroughly when he sinned

8. **Solomon:** Asked for wisdom, not riches; built for God

9. **Peter:** Learned through failure; preached fearlessly; loved to the death

10. **Paul:** Continually equipped and empowered others; patiently reinforced what he taught; corrected wrongs, disciplined, and encouraged right behavior; obeyed the Holy Spirit

11. **Jesus:** Valued everyone—no matter what the gender, social status or race; looked at the heart and discerned motives; maintained integrity; was uncompromising with His message; did only what God told Him to do; forgave and loved well; ministered in the gifts of the Holy Spirit and exhibited the fruit of the Holy Spirit; gave His life for his friends; fulfilled the mission

CHECKUP QUESTIONS TO ASK MYSELF AS A LEADER:

1. Am I serving in my area of gifting? Does what I do make my heart "sing?"

2. Besides leading, do I demonstrate a lifestyle of love for those in my personal life and neighborhood as well as in the ministry?

3. Am I raising up the next generation of leaders by empowering others who are gifted to do what I am doing and more?

4. Do I think in terms of "team," or am I a solo player? Am I willing to resource other leaders to enrich my leading?

5. Do I show respect for my authorities, whether I agree with them or not?

6. Have any of my staff members become too dependent upon me as mentor or counselor? Do I need help setting them free to think for themselves and use what I have taught them? Do I need help setting boundaries?

7. Am I possessive of what I do? Do I get my identity from it? Would I gladly give it to another leader for a season, or permanently, if asked to do so?

8. Are there any unresolved hurts in my heart from the past that sometimes steal my joy? To whom can I go for counseling?

9. Have I asked a wise person to watch my life and hold me accountable for personal growth? How do I feel about being corrected?

10. Is my devotional life strong and rewarding? Do I practice solitude in order to hear God?

11. Do I have committed intercessors to support me and to do spiritual warfare on behalf of those I influence?

12. Am I being mentored by (or seeking to learn from) someone more seasoned in leading than I am?

Scriptures: II Tim. 2:2; Eph. 4:11-13; Phil. 2:1-4; Col. 3:12-16; I Thess. 5:14

YEAR END REVIEW QUESTIONS TO ASK YOUR MINISTRY PERSONEL:

1. Are you spending quality time daily in prayer and the Word?

2. Do you pursue solitude with God?

3. What is your Personal Growth Plan for the next six months?

4. In what capacity were you most used by God this year?

5. In what area do you wish you had done more? What do you wish you had done differently?

6. What goals for your ministry were accomplished?

7. What dreams remain unfulfilled?

8. In what ways did God minister *to you* the most during this past year? What did you learn about yourself in the process? How has it changed your relationship with God?

9. How will that affect your ministry?
10. What percentage of your ministry time is spent in the area of your strongest gifting?

11. What functions annoy you because they draw on your weakest abilities? How would you like your ministry description changed to enable you to increase your level of effectiveness?

12. If you had a magic wand, what would you change about this ministry organization?

13. What training would have made your work easier? Did you always have the material or tools you needed to get your job done?

14. How can I help you become a more effective in your ministry as a developing leader?

15. What do you enjoy most about serving on this ministry team?

16. Do you have any questions or comments for me in particular? If so, what are they?

17. How may I pray for you?

RECOMMENDED READING ON LEADERSHIP:

- *Christian Coaching*, by Gary R. Collins, PH.D. NavPress, 2001.
- *Church Leadership*, by Lovett H. Weems, Jr. Abingdon Press, 1993.
- *Developing the Leader Within You*, by John Maxwell. Thomas Nelson, 1993.
- *Developing the Leaders Around You*, by John Maxwell
- *In the Name of Jesus*, by Henri J. M. Nouwen. Crossroad Pub. Co., 1998.
- *Instruments for His Glory*, by Joyce Strong. Creation House, 1999.
- *Jesus CEO*, by Laurie Beth Jones. Hyperion, 1995.
- *Lambs on the Ledge*, by Joyce Strong. CPI, 1995.
- *Leaders,* by Warren Bennis and Burt Nanus. Harper Business, 1997.
- *Leadership Without Easy Answers*, by Ronald A. Heifetz. Belknap Harvard, 1994.
- *Leading and Managing Your Church*, by Carl F. George and Robert E. Logan. Revell, 1987.
- *Lincoln on Leadership*, by Donald T. Phillips. Warner Books,

1992.
- *Mentoring,* by Bobb Biehl. Broadman & Holman Pub., 1996.
- *Of Dreams and Kings and Mystical Things*, by Joyce Strong. Destiny Image, 2002.
- *Spirit at Work,* by Jay Conger & Assoc. Jossey Bass, 1994.
- *Spiritual Leadership*, by J. Oswald Sanders. Moody Press, 1994.
- *The Making of a Christian Leader*, by Ted Engstrom. Zondervan, 1976.
- *21 Irrefutable Laws of Leadership*, by John Maxwell.
- *Upside Down*, by Stacy T. Rinehart. NavPress, 1998.
- *Values Driven Leadership*, by Aubrey Malphurs. Baker Books, 1992.